An Inside Mountie

Adventures of the First Woman Mountie. Book 14

LAURIE SCHRAMM

This book is a work of historical fiction, set in the 1970s. Although most of the historical references are accurate, a few are not, and names, characters, places, and incidents are either the product of the author's imagination or are used fictitiously. Any resemblance to actual persons, living or dead is entirely coincidental.

Print ISBN: 978-1-0690565-2-8
ePub ISBN: 978-1-0690565-3-5

Laurie Schramm

Espionage Rules

TOP ~~SECRET~~
~~SECRET~~
CONFIDENTIAL

1. Betrayal may come from within,
2. Assume nothing,
3. Stay consistent over time,
4. Keep your options open,
5. Never go against your gut,
6. Don't look back, you are not alone,
7. Go with the flow; blend in,
8. Use misdirection and deception,
9. Do not harass the opposition,
10. Lull them into complacency,
11. Pick the time and place for action,
12. Remember Murphy's Law.

(See Endnote 1)

Laurie Schramm

DEDICATION

To the women and men of Canada's real-life security-intelligence services (1864 - Present).

Laurie Schramm

CONTENTS

Laurie Schramm

ACKNOWLEDGMENTS

I am extremely grateful to the growing number of friendly readers that that have provided encouragement, comments, and suggestions based on drafts of these books: Ann Marie, Katherine, Victoria, William, Dawson, Al, Jayme, Karen M., and Ernie.

Special thanks also to five real-life veterans of the RCMP, all of whom have supplemented their encouragement with background, advice, and factual reference materials on the Force: Chief Superintendent William Schramm (Ret.), who also kindly allowed my main character to borrow his Regimental Number, Assistant Commissioner Dawson Hovey (Ret.), Deputy Commissioner Peter German, KC, Ph.D. (Ret.), Constable Karen Frost (Ret., one of the trailblazing women Mounties who joined-up when women represented only 2% of the total uniformed complement), and especially Staff Sergeant Al Lund (Ret., author of *Mounties on the Cover* and probably the world's leading authority on Mountie fiction).

Laurie Schramm

LIST OF CHARACTERS
(IN ORDER OF APPEARANCE)

- Major Jack Evans, Defence Attaché, British High Commission
- Corporal Alexandra (Alex) Houston, RCMP Security Service
- Silver, an Alaskan Malamute; and Alex's friend and police-service-dog partner
- Staff Sergeant Robert (Bob) Simpson, RCMP Security Service
- Deputy Commissioner George MacLeod
- Mary MacLeod, George's wife
- Rear-Admiral Peter White, head of the Canadian Forces Security Branch.
- Captain Donald (Don) Harrison, Military Intelligence, Canadian Armed Forces
- Staff Sergeant Avery Blunt, RCMP Security Service
- Special Agent Vivian Rule, FBI
- Staff Sergeant Alexander Demeniak, RCMP Security Service
- Sergeant Frank Wilson, Military Intelligence, Canadian Forces
- Lieutenant Sandy Moore, Military Intelligence, Canadian Forces
- Ginger Brandt, Canadian TV and film actress
- Major Emilis (Emi) Matulis, Chief Military Attaché, Embassy of the Soviet Union, Ottawa
- 'C,' head of the British Secret Intelligence Service (MI6)
- Constable Jack McDonald, RCMP
- Constable Chris Williams, RCMP

LIST OF ACRONYMS AND ABBREVIATIONS

AECL   Atomic Energy of Canada Limited
CANDU   CANadian Deuterium Uranium (nuclear reactor system)
CFB   Canadian Forces Base
HMCS   Her Majesty's Canadian Ship
HQ   Headquarters
IDENT   Identification (or Forensic) Services
MI6   Military Intelligence Sect. 6 (the UK's Secret Intelligence
        Service)
OPP   Ontario Provincial Police
PDS   Police Dog Service
PSD   Police Service Dog
RCAF   Royal Canadian Air Force
RCMP   Royal Canadian Mounted Police
USAF   Unites States Air Force
USCGC   United States Coast Guard Cutter

1 THEIRS NOT TO REASON WHY[2]

'Black Friday'
February 20, 1959
Ottawa, Ontario

The Right Honourable John G. Diefenbaker, Prime Minister of
Canada, rose in the House of Commons to give a speech[3]:

> "Mr. Speaker, with the leave of the house I should like to
> make a somewhat lengthy statement on the subject of one
> facet of the national defence of Canada.... The announcement
> I wish to make has to do with the decision regarding our air
> defence.... The government has carefully examined and re-
> examined the probable need for the Arrow aircraft and
> Iroquois engine known as the CF-105.... The conclusion
> arrived at is that the development of the Arrow aircraft and
> Iroquois engine should be terminated now."

With that simple announcement, Canada's program to build a
nuclear-weapon capable, long-range, all-weather, supersonic
interceptor came to an abrupt end. The plane was named Avro
Arrow, and the new engines that would propel it to speeds of Mach
2 (twice the speed of sound), were named Iroquois. The Arrow had
been conceived in response to growing apprehensions about the
probability of the Soviet Union developing a supersonic,

1

intercontinental bomber coupled with an assessment that no other country, at the time, had a jet fighter capable of intercepting such aircraft with the speed and range needed to protect Canada's vast land mass.

As soon as the Prime Minister's announcement had been made, the Department of Defence Production notified Avro Canada, the primary contractor on the program, that the program was cancelled and that they were to immediately cease all work. With all funding cut off, the company had little choice but to shut down its operations that same afternoon, throwing more than 25,000 people out of work: 14,000 Avro Aircraft and Orenda Engines employees, and more than 11,000 at various sub-contractors.

The news media, of course, launched into a frenzy of questions, assertions, and speculations about the wisdom of the government's decision, and the reason(s) it had been made. The latter ranged from budgetary considerations (the official reason), to undue influence from the United States (whether due to politics, their own defence policies, or simply pride)[4]. Not the least of the concerns expressed was whether there would be any return from the over $300 million[5] that had already been spent on the Avro program by the time of the cancellation order.

From *The (Toronto) Telegram*, February 21, 1959.

Within months, orders were given to scrap the five flyable aircraft plus those under construction[6], all but three of the engines, and the rest of the parts, jigs, documents, and so forth, saving only one complete set of drawings, specifications, manuals, and the like[5].

By January of 1960, Avro had been ordered to destroy the balance of the documentation[5]. For security reasons, the government wanted to make sure that no other country would be able to make the Arrow either (although in later years several countries 'reinvented' some of the Arrow's most advanced features, including the internal weapons carriage, and the fly-by-wire power-assist for the controls while in supersonic flight).

> In the fields of observation chance favours only the prepared mind.
>
> Louis Pasteur, French microbiologist/chemist,
> During a lecture at the University of Lille,
> 7 December 1854

Sunday, May 10, 1959
Mississauga, Ontario

In a rented aviation-hanger on Airport Road, not far from the manufacturing facilities of Avro Aircraft and Orenda Engines, all the lights were still on despite it being late in the evening. Inside the nearly empty hangar were stacks of irregularly-sized cardboard boxes. Next to the boxes was a large and disorderly pile of documents. That the documents had been unceremoniously dumped from other boxes could fairly be deduced from the third pile, which comprised empty boxes that had been flattened and tossed aside.

Beyond the boxes and documents, the only noteworthy things were in a noisy corner where two men toiled away. Other than that, the hanger was empty and quiet: it was the night shift on a Sunday, and there was no one else around except the security guards at the front door.

The noise in the corner where the men were working and the pervading, almost intolerable smell of machine oil, came from two sturdy-looking industrial paper shredders[7]. The men were hand-feeding documents to the shredders which, notwithstanding the machine oil, frequently overheated and jammed. When this happened, the machines had to be turned off, opened-up, and allowed to cool, while the men used pliers to free the cutting blades from the jammed tangles of paper.

There was a recurring debate between the two men about which was the more tedious: the monotonous feeding of documents into the jaws of the shredders or the frustrating job of freeing the jammed blades.

It would be an understatement to say that the men were unenthusiastic about their work. They were surrounded by piles of documents from the cancelled Avro Arrow program; mostly test reports, drawings, specifications, manuals, and the like. A few were stamped CONFIDENTIAL, others were stamped SECRET, and most of them were stamped TOP SECRET.

It was boring, menial work, and they had been at it for hours with no end in sight. Since the documents were being destroyed for security reasons, they could only be handled by people with Top Secret, or higher, security clearances. In this case, both men had Top Secret security clearance, and both men acutely felt the indignity of having to do a job they felt was beneath them.

"Look at this," said one of the men, in a tone of disgust. "The government spends over 300 million dollars developing the best fighter jet in the world, and now we're helping to destroy it all. What a waste!"

"Well, it's all pensionable time, as they say," replied the second, more philosophical of the two.

"But why? That's what I don't get. Even if the program became too expensive, there are rumours that the British offered to buy the design from us. Why not just sell it to them instead of all this?"

The second man, who had been about to say 'Ours not to reason why,' stopped himself to instead say: "The British are interested? I didn't know that."

"That's what I heard. You know Frank over in B Section[8]? He told me yesterday that the British called and were interested in buying or licensing Arrows for long-range defence over the North Sea[9]."

"Huh. What do you know about that?" said the second man, thoughtfully. As this was a purely rhetorical expression, the first man didn't say anything further, and the two men went back to their shredding.

After another hour of relentless shredding, a telephone rang and they switched off the shredders so the first man could answer it.

"Hello? Yes, that's me, put her on.

"Hi Honey, what's up? No, no, slow down. Stop and take a breath; I can't understand a word you're saying.

"Ok. Yes, that's better.... What!! Now? You're sure? Ok, ok, I get it. I'll be there as fast as I can. You get your coat on and get that bag you packed. I'll be right there."

"Trouble?" asked the second man, after the first had hung up the phone and taken a deep breath.

"Yes and no. That was my wife. She says she's gone into labour. She keeps saying something about water breaking."

"Your first?"

"Yes.... Look, I need to ask a big favour."

"You want to go take her to the hospital and you want me to cover for you. Right?"

"Yes. Look, I know we were ordered to only do this together, with each of us watching the other for security reasons, but it's stupid, for God's sake. I mean, look at us, we're on the same side – we're both Mounted Policemen, so we're even on the same team. It won't take me long to slip out, go pick her up, drop her off at the hospital[10], and then come straight back here. Two hours at the most. Then, if you keep on shredding while I'm gone, and the two of us keep going after that, we'll still get enough done on this shift and no one will be the wiser."

"Sure. Go ahead. I'll cover for you," said the second man, "but make sure you go out the back way so the front-desk people don't see you."

"Thanks. I owe you one," said the first man gratefully, as he headed for the door.

Alone in the room, the second man picked up one of the manuals. "January 1959. AIRCRAFT OPERATING INSTRUCTIONS – ARROW 1. Avro Aircraft limited," read the label on the cover[11]. It was over 140 pages. *Everything a pilot needs to know to fly one of these*, he thought, as he flipped through it

He picked up another manual, then another. *Everything someone would need to build and maintain one of these*, he thought, as he flipped through several of the specification books and manuals. When he reached over to pull another manual out of the pile, a box of technical reports that was sitting on top fell over to reveal a very thick wad of blueprints, held together on one edge by a wooden frame. As he flipped through the blueprints, his jaw dropped, and he paused to gaze around the various piles.

There's enough material here to build, operate, and maintain a fleet of Avro Arrows, he thought.

Structural Drawing of the Arrow Mk. I, Avro Canada

***

Two weeks later.
Ottawa, Ontario

In a large, eight-story building, directly across the street from the National Arts Centre in downtown Ottawa the morning routine was just getting started when a call was received on the main telephone line.

"Good morning, British High Commission," said a woman's voice belonging to one of the main switchboard operators.

"Major Evans, please," said man's voice. The voice sounded muffled, and there was crackling on the line, but it was possible to understand his request.

"One moment please. I'll connect you."

There was a click on the line, a pause, and then another click.

"Defence Liaison," said a new woman's voice.

The caller repeated his request.

"Who may I say is calling?"

"Just tell him it's a *friend*[12]," said the voice, with heavy emphasis on the last word.

"One moment please. I'll see if he can take your call."

There was a another click on the line as it was put on hold, a longer pause this time, and then another click as a handset was picked up.

"Major Evans speaking."

"You can call me Smith, Major Evans. I have something that I think will interest you very much."

"What might that be, Mr. Smith?"

"Just Smith, if you please. I understand that you have an interest in long-range, supersonic jet fighters for use over the North Sea and elsewhere."

"Possibly. We do try to keep abreast of things you know," Major Evans, said, cautiously.

"Indeed. What if I could supply you with the plans for the Avro Arrow and its supersonic engines?"

"The Arrow was cancelled. Didn't I read somewhere that everything was being destroyed?"

"Possibly, but you shouldn't believe everything that you read, you know."

"Well, then, what do you have?"

"Everything but the planes themselves. Materials lists, assembly instructions, blueprints[13], maintenance instructions, service manuals, wind-tunnel test results, weapons systems specifications... even operating instructions."

"I see, and am I to assume that these are all for sale?"

"You are."

"Hmmm. What do you want?"

"Not much. Let's say five-hundred thousand. That wouldn't be much to pay for three-hundred-million worth of technology. Not when there's enough information to build as many jets as you want. It would be worth it just for the engines alone. Wouldn't it?"

There was a pause. Then, "I'll have to get approval, and we'll need some kind of evidence."

"Of course. Across the street from you is the National Arts Centre. In the box office lobby is a wire-frame news-stand with free neighbourhood and religious newspapers. At the back of the papers in the upper-left corner, you will find three samples. Get one of your experts to look over the samples, get approval for the money, and I'll phone you again in a week."

A week later, another call was received at the High Commission for Major Evans.

"Well?"

"The documents check out. We're interested."

"All right. We won't meet. We'll use dead drops[14]. Put 150 thousand into a briefcase. Used, unmarked bills, in small denominations. I'll phone in two days with instructions. When I get the money, I'll phone again and tell you where to get the first large batch of documents. They will be in two large suitcases. After that we'll repeat the process. Then, for the last cycle, it will be the remaining 200 thousand dollars, in return for which you'll get the only surviving, complete set of original blueprints."

Over the next two weeks, the three rounds of exchanges of money and documents took place. Every exchange took place at a different pair of dead drops. A few days after the final exchange, Major Evans received another call at the High Commission.

"You have everything?"

"Yes."

"And you are satisfied?"

"Yes. Do you have anything else for us?"

"Not now, but sometime in the future, I may call you again."

"Cheers."

That went well, thought the security man.

2 A VERY ODD CALL

> *Quis custodiet ipsos custodes* (who watches the watchers)?
>
> From *Satires of Juvenal*, (Satire 6, 346-348)
>
> Rome, *Circa.* 100

October, 1980
Ottawa, Ontario

"E007, 10-21," the radio in my truck crackled to life.

My name is Corporal Alexandra Houston, Royal Canadian Mounted Police (RCMP) Security Service. My friends call me Alex. E007 was the call-sign assigned to my radio. The letter E designated my unit as operational support. This prefix was assigned to unmarked police-dog-service (PDS) or forensic (IDENT) units. In my case I'm also a dog master and I always travel with Silver, an Alaskan Malamute, my friend and partner. The number '007' showed that my boss, Staff Sergeant Robert (Bob) Simpson, Bob had a sense of humour (he often jokes that I'm like a female James Bond). As if my Security Service posting didn't give me enough variety, we were often called out in our capacity as a PDS team.

"E007," I acknowledged.

"Message for you from Staff Sergeant Simpson. Message reads: 'Phone in when convenient. Not urgent.'"

That was odd. My boss Bob wouldn't have gone through the radio room to contact me if it wasn't important, so I took his message to mean fairly urgent but not an emergency.

"E007, 10-4," I responded over the radio, meaning that I was acknowledging receipt of the message and that I would handle it 'as requested.'

I was driving along an Ottawa street, heading for one of the main highways at the time. Looking ahead, I spotted a phone booth in the corner of a service station's parking lot and pulled in to make the call.

Pushing a coin in to the appropriate slot, I received a dial tone and punched in the number for the RCMP's Ottawa radio room. When it was answered, I identified myself, read-out the number on the pay phone, and explained that I'd received a radio message to phone in. The duty officer replied that he'd pass my message on and we hung up. I didn't expect to be kept waiting long, and I was right. Within a few minutes the phone rang.

"Alex?" came a familiar voice over the phone.

"Hi Bob. What's up?"

"Where are you now and what are you doing today?"

"Well, I was working on the Strangways case until a request came in from the OPP[15] for me to help them on a search. Their own dog teams are either fully engaged or out of the area. I was just on my way out of town, heading for Highway 416 and Kemptville."

"Ah. Good. So, you won't be far away." Kemptville was about 60 km (36 miles) south of Ottawa, so about a 40-minute drive.

"I have news," he continued. "Uncle George was on today's promotion list. He's being bumped up to Deputy Commissioner." Uncle George was Bob's and my unofficial and top-secret codename for (formerly) Assistant Commissioner George MacLeod, the head of the Security Service and Bob's boss. Others on the staff referred to him as 'The Old Man,' the same as if he was the CO of a Division, but Bob and I referred to him as Uncle George. We always figured that if we were ever found out, we'd claim it was a code name for security reasons, but it was really because he looked after us like family.

"Deputy Commissioner! That's great. It's overdue, but it's

great."

"Right. His job title is still Director General of the Security Service, but it's always been a Deputy Commissioner-level position[16]. He was pretty young when he came into the role, so this is a kind of recognition that he's been doing a good job. Anyway, he's having a few people over this evening for come-and-go cocktails at his house and you're invited."

I hesitated. "Isn't that a bit high-brow? I imagine his friends in the Force are senior officers. The Ottawa ones anyway."

"Well, that's true enough, quite a few of the top brass and their wives will be there, but there'll be a few token non-comms[17] like you and I there as well."

I hesitated again. "I'm not sure when I'll be able to get back into town, you know."

"Yes, I mentioned that possibility to him but he said he'd be particularly pleased if you'd come, and that when you go off duty just head over to his house dressed as you are – no need to clean up, and no need to change into civilian clothes."

That sounded suspicious to me but, in practice, a politely-phrased request from a senior officer wasn't much different from a direct order, so I agreed. "What about Silver?" I asked.

"Well, I asked him that too, and he said, 'Tell her to bring Silver too. She never goes anywhere without him anyway'"

I had to chuckle at that. He'd said more or less the same thing to me more than once in the years I'd been indirectly working for him. "OK," I relented. "I'll be there, but I'll still clean up and change clothes first if there's time."

"Fair enough," said Bob. "I'll see you there. In the meantime, good luck with the OPP and your search."

As I rung off it still seemed odd to me, to be invited to a Deputy Commissioner's promotion party. I had a huge amount of respect for 'Uncle George,' and I was pleased to be invited, but it still seemed... odd. I forced it to the back of my mind as I went back to my unmarked police SUV and resumed course for Kemptville and its OPP detachment.

The search, turned out to be for the escape route used by a thief who'd broken into a farmhouse and stolen a pair of valuable handguns. This wasn't the sort of thing we'd normally be called out to, except for some unusual circumstances. The break-in had been very recent, perhaps only an hour or two earlier, the pistols were both functional and loaded, and the thief had left a piece of clothing behind. Apparently, the thief had gotten their jacket caught in the barbs of a barbed-wire fence while getting away, and the local police thought there might be an opportunity to catch the thief while still in possession of the guns.

We'd done this kind of searching many times before, so after letting Silver get a good sniff of the jacket, I simply set him off to search. In company with us were an OPP sergeant and two constables. Silver set about doing his thing, and we followed along as his zig-zagging sniffing led us to a wind-break stand of trees, then along a narrow creek-bed, and finally to a neighbouring field and a rough, narrow dirt road that could have been the wagon-road of a hundred years earlier. The scent trail ended at a spot to one side of the road, where fresh-looking tire tracks indicated a vehicle had been parked. From the size of the tread marks and the spacing between them, the sergeant concluded that a full-size pickup truck had been parked there. While these were being examined, Silver had meandered off to investigate some nearby bushes, after which he gave a sharp bark, sat down on his haunches, and looked expectantly at me.

"What'd you find Silver?" I asked, as I walked over. He looked pointedly down to one side, and there, in the scrub, was a cheap backpack. Closer investigation showed that it contained a rather heavy, polished mahogany box.

"Find something?" asked the sergeant, who had noticed us and come over to see for himself.

"Were the guns in a presentation case, by chance?" I asked.

"They were, and that looks like the description we were given." Pulling on a pair of gloves, he carefully removed the box from the backpack and eased open the two latches. There was nothing inside but the moulded depressions in the felt that would have held the two guns: revolvers from the shape of the depressions. Closing the case, he turned it this way and that, looking at the outer surfaces. "Looks like some nice prints here. We'll get them taken and run through your database. Maybe we'll be lucky and get a hit."

The other officers had more work to do, but it was clear that Silver and I had done all we could so, with their thanks for our help, we walked back to the original farm and our truck where I wrote everything up in my notebook in case we should be called sometime later to testify in court.

That done, I sighed and checked my watch. I was pleased that we'd helped enough to give the officers some clues, and a fighting chance to eventually catch their thief, but it was pretty routine and hardly qualified as one of our more exciting cases. It was, however, getting late. Uncle George's promotion social was scheduled for 7 to 10 pm, and it was already past 8. There was no way I'd be able to get home, clean up, change clothes and get over there in time. If I was going to go at all, I would have to drive straight there. As I looked down at the tactical uniform I was wearing, it brought new meaning to the term 'come as you are.' My boots were dirty, of course, but beyond that my uniform still looked pretty clean. *Oh well*, I thought, *he asked for it.* And I did want to honour his invitation and congratulate him.

Deputy Commissioner George MacLeod lived in Rockcliffe Park, a very historic and prestigious neighbourhood that is quite close to the centre of Ottawa. It was originally a small village, having been established in the mid-1800s, but eventually became amalgamated into the city of Ottawa. It contains many stately homes, with beautiful yards and mature trees and, of course, was inhabited by some of Ottawa's elite, and I slowed down a bit as I drove past Stornoway, a beautiful three-story period home owned by the federal government and operated as the residence of the leader of the Official Opposition. As I passed it, I couldn't help wondering whether Joe Clark[18] was in residence at that moment. The MacLeods lived a few blocks away, in a smaller but otherwise similar 19th-century house.

"Well Silver, this should be an experience for us," I said, as we got out of the truck and walked up to the front door.

When I rang the doorbell, I wasn't sure quite what to expect, but I was surprised when the door was opened by the Deputy Commissioner himself.

"Alex!" he said, with a big smile, "and Silver too, I see."

I instinctively stiffened to attention and saluted even though, strictly speaking, I needn't have as he was dressed in civilian clothes.

He nodded in acknowledgement, but said: "Now, now. At ease Alex. That's more than enough formality for tonight, thank you. I'm pleased you could come. Welcome to our home." Turning to look back into the house, he bellowed in a full, parade-ground voice: "Mary! Come see who's here!"

"I'm sorry about my appearance, Sir, but Staff-Sergeant Simpson said to come straight from work if necessary, and Silver and I just finished a search near Kemptville then came directly here."

"Don't worry about it, I'm just glad you were able to make it. Mary, I'd like you to meet someone." This last was directed at a woman who'd arrived at his shoulder. As he stepped aside, he said: "This is Alex Houston and her partner Silver. Alex, my wife Mary."

"How do you do Ma'am," I said, tipping my head deferentially.

"Alex?" she said, raising an eyebrow.

"Short for Alexandra Ma'am."

"Well, it's a pleasure to meet you Alexandra," she said, offering a hand to shake, "and you too Silver," she said, looking directly into his eyes.

"*Grruph*," said Silver, gazing directly back at her with a slightly inquisitive look. That broke the ice, and had everyone chuckling.

"You must call me Mary," she said, "none of that Ma'am stuff. It makes me feel old and stuffy. Now come inside and let's get you freshened up before you have to meet anyone else."

As we stepped inside, I paused to remove my boots and leave them – and my hat - in the entrance vestibule. Then, I was whisked upstairs to what was clearly Mary's bedroom, which had a beautiful Victorian-era makeup desk and mirror, and an attached bathroom.

"Don't worry about your uniform, but if you'd like to wash your face and run a comb through your hair, I'll see if I can find a pair of slippers for you that won't clash too much with your uniform trousers."

Thanking her, I set about to make 'emergency repairs' which didn't amount to much because my hair is fairly short, I don't normally wear any makeup, and didn't have any with me anyway. It did feel good to wash my face in warm water and run a comb through my hair though.

I'd just finished when Mary returned with a pair of handmade leather moccasins and pulled out a chair to sit on. The moccasins actually fit me reasonably well. "Very appropriate," I commented and thanked her.

"Well, you look better already," she commented, looking me over. Then, she reached out a hand towards my hair, saying: "may I?"

I nodded, and she gently ran her fingers through my red hair.

"It's too bad, your job won't let you grow it out," she said. "I'd give anything to have rich, thick hair like yours. It's your natural colour too, isn't it? It matches your green eyes and fair complexion beautifully. Your appearance isn't what I'd imagined at all.

"I know a lot about you, you see. George told me all about convincing you to leave the Toronto Police and join the Force, and how you and Silver first met – it must have been terrifying – and some of your adventures. He doesn't tell me the really secret parts, of course, but he hints at them, and the parts he has shared sound like they could have come out of adventure novels."

"Well, I've been very lucky," I replied. "I wanted adventure, I've been able to do the kind of work I love, and I've been able to survive too. So far, at least."

"Yes, you seem to have experienced more action in the past six or seven years than most officers see in an entire career. George is very proud of you, you know. He might not ever tell you to your face, but you can take it from me."

I blushed. "That's very kind."

"Well now," she said, deftly changing the subject. "Before we go and mingle, I'd like to explain a little bit about a side of the Force's culture that you may not have encountered before."

As I nodded, she pulled up another chair.

"You know better than I that the Force is still a male-dominated, paramilitary organization. Even with new women coming in each year, only one in ten of the new constables are women. That means culture change is coming, but it will take decades before there is any kind of gender equality within the ranks. Naturally, many of our friends are within the Force, and of our own generation. That means, when we go downstairs to mingle, you're going to find that all of the other women are spouses from an earlier generation, leaving you as the only woman who is a serving Member.

"On top of that, most of the men downstairs are senior officers. That's OK, you already know how to deal with them. But there's a kind of society among the wives that has its own hierarchy determined by the ranks of the women's husbands. Understand?"

"I suppose so. Presumably, it's the same in the military."

"Probably so. It's tempered a bit here in Ottawa, because our circle merges with those of the rich, and the politicians, and the diplomats, but it still exists. My only point is that you will be something of a novelty, and a very junior novelty in terms of rank. Everyone will be superficially nice tonight because of the setting but, underneath, some of them will be uncomfortable because they won't quite know where you fit in."

"Yes. Or if I fit in at all," I mused.

"I'm afraid so. I just thought I should warn you in advance."

"All right. Thank you. I think I'm as ready as I'm going to be, if you'd like to go down."

So, we went down, and Mary walked me over to a small group of people, introduced me, and then moved on to complete other hostly duties.

Then, periodically, after a few minutes she would come rescue me and introduce me to another group, and so on. Before long, I had met most of the people there and I was amazed at how efficiently, yet discreetly, she had managed it all. Everyone was very polite, and in many cases asked where I had grown up, and where I had been previously posted. I soon learned that almost everyone was originally from other parts of the country and that I was one of the few that had actually grown up in Ontario.

As Mary had predicted, everyone was polite and friendly. At least on the surface. But it wasn't exactly enjoyable and certainly not relaxing. A fair number of the women seemed rather condescending and, behind my back I heard a few whispering words to the effect that the Force had been crazy to begin letting women in. I did my best to pretend not to hear them, and to ignore them. Silver, perceptive as always, was tense and I had no doubt that he detected the unstated moods, and my reactions to them.

I reminded myself that I'd faced worse on my cases, like being shot at and nearly drowning or crashing in aircraft, and so on, but that didn't help as much as it should have. I guess we all share an inner desire to be liked. Having Mary move me around from group to group did make it easier for me, though, and I survived.

It was probably around 9:30 pm when the tinkling of a glass bell was used to call for order, and a distinguished looking man wearing a dark suit asked for a moment of everyone's attention.

"The Commissioner himself, no less," said a voice behind me. Although I turned to look, I'd immediately recognized the voice of Bob, my immediate boss.

"Hi Bob," I whispered, "when did you get here?"

16

"Just now. I was detained."

The Commissioner offered just a few remarks, in which he praised the new Deputy Commissioner's career and recent work leading the Security Service and said he looked forward to future great things from him. Although brief, I thought that his remarks carried a sense of genuineness and conviction.

For his part, Uncle George followed up with some nice words of thanks and appreciation for the opportunities he'd been given, reminded us that no one accomplishes great things all by themselves, and said some very complimentary things about the men and women it had been his pleasure to work with, and his honour to lead. His final words were: "The military have a saying: 'look after your troops, and your troops will look after you.' I've always felt it is quite appropriate."

"And *that*, is why most of us would follow him to the gates of Hell and back," said Bob, *sotto voce*.

I nodded in agreement. I felt that way too.

"By the way," continued Bob in a whisper, "don't rush off at ten o'clock with everyone else. Uncle George would like a quiet word with you before you go, but not while everyone else is still here."

I looked at him in surprise, but all he did was tip his head slightly down and tap the side of his nose with a forefinger.

"Corporal Houston, I believe," said a new voice behind me. This one, I did not recognize. When I turned, I was surprised to see who it was.

"Commissioner, Sir," I said, coming to attention.

"Relax, Houston. We're off duty here, although I see that you've been on duty more recently than the rest of us," he said, looking at my uniform with a chuckle. "No, no, you don't need to explain," he added, correctly discerning that I was about to apologize for having showed up in uniform. "George told me that you were off lending a helping hand to the OPP and only recently escaped to join us here." He looked down. "And this must be your partner, Silver. Hello Silver!" He carefully knelt down on one knee, held out a hand for Silver to sniff, and looked him straight in the eye.

Silver, having given him a sound sniffing, and a penetrating stare, decided the Commissioner was OK and relaxed.

"I think I just passed an inspection there," said the Commissioner. "It's probably just as well. I don't think I'd like to meet him alone on a dark night if he took an active dislike to me."

"No Sir. The first time I met him, it was in the dark, and I thought he was a wolf. When he snarled at me, it felt like every hair on my body was standing on end!"

"I don't doubt it. Is it OK if I offer him a dog treat?" he asked, rummaging in one of his suit pockets.

"Yes Sir, but please don't be offended if he doesn't take it. I've only seen him accept food from a stranger once and that was from my future fiancé."

"Ah yes, the good Captain Harrison. I've been hearing about him lately too.... Ah, here we go. I have two dogs myself, so I usually have a little something for them in my pockets. Used to carry a few lumps of sugar around with me too, in the old days, for the horses." He gave another low chuckle. "It took a while for my old troop-mates to figure out why the horses we were training with seemed to like me so much, but it was simple. I bribed them with sugar. Worked like a charm.... Here Silver. Would you like a dog biscuit?"

Silver, for his part, stunned me by gently grasping the dog biscuit with his front teeth, devouring it in a flash, and then looking up at us both with his mouth open and his tongue out in a wolfish grin.

"See what I mean?" said the Commissioner. "The Force is like one very large family. It was a pleasure to meet you Houston, George has told me quite a lot about you over the past couple of years, so I wanted to take the opportunity to meet you for myself."

As I thanked him, he strolled away, still chuckling quietly to himself.

"What do you think?" said a familiar voice. Bob had quietly materialized behind me again.

"Interesting. I sensed power and humanity at the same time. I think Silver did too. How can he possibly even know I exist? And he even seemed to know something about Don."

"Well, he can't know everything about everybody, of course, but he keeps up-to-date on the things he believes are important.... Excuse me, I see someone over there I need to speak with before this evening wraps up. Don't forget to stick around."

And with that, he was gone again, before I could ask him any more questions.

It wasn't much later that people began leaving, and soon there was a steady stream of people saying good-night and leaving. Mary came by to ask whether Silver might like some water, and led us to the kitchen for that purpose, so that by the time we re-entered the living room, everyone seemed to be gone.

Mary took this as a cue, saying "I have a confession to make. I delayed you purposely while everyone else left. George would like a word with you in his study, if you don't mind."

"Of course not," I replied, and she led me down a short hallway to the study, which was in a back corner of the house. She opened the door for me, and then closed it behind us after Silver and I had walked in.

The Deputy Commissioner was there, of course, looking more relaxed now that he'd removed his suit jacket and untied his tie and collar-button. With him was another man who was standing in one corner with his back to me, looking out one of the windows into the back yard. This second man was older, thinner, and not quite as erect in his bearing. I didn't recognize him from the back, but I could tell from his manner that Silver did. *Stranger and stranger,* I thought.

Before I could say anything, the study door opened again to admit a young man in a suit, who closed it behind him, and then walked in. He first gave a nod to Bob, and then looked at the Deputy Commissioner and said: "I just made the rounds of the whole security detail. All clear, Sir."

"Thank you," he said, and the man left, again shutting the door behind him.

"Thank you too, for staying behind for a moment, Alex. Please have a seat and get comfortable."

I sat with, perhaps, a hint of a frown.

If I did give a hint of a frown, he caught it immediately. "You've deduced that there's something unusual afoot, of course, and you're wondering why we would have a security detail covering the house and, in short, what the hell this is all about."

It was a statement, not a question, but I answered anyway. "Yes, Sir."

"It's a matter of national security, my dear," said the man in the corner.

I *did* know that voice!

"Admiral. Sir. I didn't see you out there tonight."

"No, you didn't, because I wasn't out there, and as far as anyone is ever going to know, I'm not here right now, either," said Rear-Admiral Peter White, head of the Canadian Forces Security Branch. We had met before, and I knew him to be a close friend of Uncle George and the boss of my fiancé Don, who was a Captain in Military Intelligence.

"Nice to see you again," he continued. "I hear you're going to marry one of my best intelligence operatives."

"Yes Sir."

"Good for you. He's a fine young man.... Now then, to business." He began rubbing his hands briskly, as he collected his thoughts. "I won't mince words. We have a problem."

I waited, but it was the Deputy Commissioner that spoke next.

"You've survived some extremely dangerous assignments in the past, but this one could make them look like a walk in the park. My conscience tells me that I can't ask you to take this one on, but my sense of duty says that I have to ask you exactly that, if you know what I mean."

"It's OK, Sir. If you really believe that it's me, that is, Silver and I that you want to send in, then whatever it is, the answer is yes. We'll take it on and do our best."

Uncle George looked so relieved that I immediately asked: "Did you really think I'd turn you down, Sir?"

"Well. Things have changed, haven't they? You're engaged now. I understand that you and Don each have inheritance income coming in from Don's late grandmother, so you probably don't need to work at all anymore, at least not because of the money. Besides, let's face it, you've cheated death more than once in some of the cases you've been on, Silver too. No one could blame you – no one could say you haven't done your bit and then some – if you decided to call it quits or wanted to shift to a desk job."

"Quits! Desk job!" I laughed and sat up straight. "Look, Sir, I was the one that left the Toronto force because I wanted to do some real policing – in the field! You gave me that opportunity. Then, when Silver and I found each other, it was you that cleared the path for us to get Silver in as a PSD, and I'll bet that took some doing on your part. And then, when you offered us the chance to transfer into the Security Service, and we took it, I found that Silver and I could take on things that I could never have previously even imagined. Silver was made for this kind of work. He loves it. And so do I. And all along you and Bob have had our backs.... So, now there's a new challenge? Count us in." I paused for a moment, and no one said anything; no one moved, and then I continued more quietly.

"You're right about one thing, of course. I can't keep on doing this forever. I don't want to die. I do want to get married. I want to have a family. I'll even want to retire someday – maybe even soon, when Silver does, because he's irreplaceable – to me anyway.

"But that day, is not today, Sir. If you want us for this, then count us in. A mutual colleague of ours recently commented that we'd follow you to the gates of Hell and back if you wanted." I avoided looking at Bob, who seemed to have found something interesting in the ceiling to look at. "I think our colleague was right."

Uncle George said... nothing. It was the first and the last time I ever saw him left speechless. It was Admiral White, that came to the rescue, with his trademark brisk manner.

"Well spoken, young woman. So," he said in anticipation, "let's get on with the planning, shall we?" He was rubbing his hands together again.

"Right," said Uncle George, regaining his composure, although it seemed to me that his eyes were a little moist.

"Have you ever heard of the Avro Arrow program?" asked the Admiral.

"Yes," I nodded, "it was going to be a supersonic fighter jet but the program was cancelled, wasn't it?"

"Indeed, in 1959 the program was scrapped and everything was ordered destroyed for security reasons. No one wanted the Soviets to be able to learn its secrets and use them against us. We weren't even allowed to transfer the know-how to the Americans, although they managed to get it all anyway, or the British, or the French, both of whom were interested. BUT," he said, smacking his hands together for emphasis, "someone acquired a complete set of the designs and manuals and sold them to the British."

There was silence in the room for a moment.

"We don't know who it was," continued the Admiral. "Both of our services knew the British got the plans, and the British knew that we knew, but it was never spoken of directly and we were ordered not to pursue it from the highest levels. They're our allies after all, it's not as if the secrets went to an unfriendly power, and our government wanted to avoid an embarrassing diplomatic incident. So, our predecessors followed orders and dropped it. But we have long memories in the intelligence business, and we never forgot that there was an insider threat somewhere. Since then, there have been a few other incidents – security breaches involving leaks of secret information - that our services were not able to quite get to the bottom of."

"You'll remember the Second World War weather station and the two East German agents you and Don caught in Nova Scotia a few years ago?" asked the Deputy Commissioner, picking up the tale.

"Vividly," I said. "1977. It involved the technology behind the plants in Cape Breton that were making heavy water for our CANDU nuclear reactors[19]."

"Right. Well, you broke up the information pipeline but we never discovered how the information was obtained in the first place."

"I remember now. Bob told me that he suspected an agent in-place somewhere, like in the plants, or at AECL[20] maybe."

"Very likely, but there may have been someone in the security and intelligence community as well, that put the pieces together, established the connections, and possibly even directed the operation. There were a few hints along those lines, but nothing actionable.

"There was also a case in the 1960s, in which an entire file disappeared that had been confiscated from a document forger. The file contained a half dozen 'legends,' complete fake identities and supporting documents that could be used to obtain Canadian passports[21]. They were sold to a broker, who was later apprehended, but the original source was never discovered.

"Well, there were a few other incidents but you get the idea. Now, it's possible that there's no connection between these incidents, but Admiral White and I think there is. The common thread is some kind of connection in either the Security Service or

Military Intelligence[22]."

"A mole, then, do you think?"

"Not in the usual sense, because the consistent theme is money, and the beneficiaries of the security breaches are so varied: enemies, allies, crooks, and even organized crime. More likely it's a lone-wolf working for himself, and only when he wants, or when opportunities present themselves every few years.

"We even had Bob here try putting out bait a few times. Bits of real intelligence, but not critical intelligence, to see if we could expose the source." He paused and looked at Bob, who gave an unhappy-looking shrug.

The Deputy Commissioner sighed, and suddenly looked very tired. "In each case, we failed. In some cases, our mysterious agent managed to outwit us and take off with the bait. In other cases, they simply didn't even try for it, as far as we know. Whether the bait was too subtle and didn't come to the agent's attention, or the agent somehow smelled a trap and steered away, well, we don't know that either.... In fact, I'm beginning to wonder some days whether we really know anything at all." He seemed to be lost in thought for a moment, then his attention snapped back and his manner became a bit more brisk.

"There's another thing. This person's motivation might not be primarily money. We're coming to the conclusion that it might just be the challenge, and possibly even the opportunity to prove to himself that he's smarter than everyone else."

"He?"

"If we're right, then the first job was in 1959. At that time, only men were highly enough placed for this kind of work. Gender equity is only beginning to creep into our culture now, twenty years later, as you well know."

"So. Someone in security and intelligence, with a high security clearance as far back as 1959," I said.

"Top Secret or better. Yes. That someone would now be in his forties, if not older."

"There can't be all that many possibilities then, can there?" I asked.

"There are at least twenty people that could possibly have had access to the various materials over the years and who are still on active duty in high-security positions. Some are in the Security Service; some are in Military Intelligence; others are in the diplomatic service. All of them have Top Secret, or better, security clearances, and all of them are supposed to be above suspicion, including Bob here and even the Admiral himself."

I think my jaw must have dropped, as the implications set in. "So. You suspect none of them, but you have to suspect all of them," I whispered.

They both nodded.

"My God! What a mess," I said, trying to think. "But… why me? I'm not in counter-intelligence, or a spy catcher, except by accident."

"Really?" challenged the Admiral. "I understand that you caught a pair of East German agents in Nova Scotia[23] in 1977, and an international arms dealer operating on the West Coast[24] later the same year, and earlier this year there was that rogue, former CIA agent in Newfoundland and Labrador[25]. Am I right?"

"Yes sir, but I didn't always know who I was chasing, or exactly what they were up to…" I trailed off, and both men smiled at me as I realized that I was inadvertently making their case for them. "And, besides," I finished, rather weakly, "I had lots of help."

"You're selling yourself short, as usual Alex," said the Deputy Commissioner. "Besides, things seem to happen around you. I don't know how you do it, but you seem to fall into the middle of things, and you've been remarkably successful so far. Look at Silver there beside you. He's astoundingly perceptive. Sometimes, I think he can actually understand what we're saying. He has done things that don't make any logical sense, that science tells us are impossible, and yet he does them over and over again, and I have no qualms about using his talents either."

"Besides," put in the Admiral, in a quiet voice. "We've tried the conventional approaches. Gone by the book, you might say. We've done it very carefully; very quietly. Bob here was part of it when he was in B Section[26]. But we've gotten nowhere. As a result, we've decided it's past time we tried something unconventional."

I couldn't repress a chuckle. "And Silver and I are still the most unconventional team in the Force?"

"Yes," said the Deputy Commissioner, with a smile, "no contest. As for help, we'll try to get you anything you need, within reason, and this time you pick your own team. OK?"

"Yes Sir."

"Fine. When you communicate with Bob, assume you are being

monitored. If you need to reach me, don't go through channels, call Mary here at home. It's simple and as secure as anything else we might dream up. This house is regularly swept for bugs and wiretaps. I'd set you up with a STU phone[27], except that they're so large it would raise questions by its very presence, and they're not portable yet either.

"I suggest that you ask Bob here for a few days leave to go visit your fiancé in Halifax. The Admiral will give Don a set of detailed notes containing a *précis* of the suspicious incidents and our attempts to get more information. Read; think; talk to Don. After that you can still back out. I won't hold it against you.

"If you're still in, then phone Bob and Mary separately, and tell them 'the game is on.' Then, pick your team and think up a cover story that will let you go off from time to time without arousing anyone's suspicions.... Any immediate questions?"

Millions, I thought. "Can I have Don?"

The Admiral nodded. They'd foreseen this, of course. "I'll give him a secure way to reach me as well," he said.

"Like I said, whomever you want, within reason. Just let us know. But don't take too long about it. All right?"

"Yes, Sir," and that was it. They thanked me, and Silver and I took our leave, pausing on the way so I could thank Mary again, for her hospitality, on the way out.

Then, having done that, Silver and I walked out in to the night air. Before we'd gone far, Bob caught up with us.

"You think Don will be OK with this?" he asked.

"Well, he'll understand at least, that's for sure."

"He's going to want to be involved, you know, if for no other reason than to try to keep an eye on you."

"Yes. I'm counting on that."

"I might have known. You're going to argue with him a bit, and then 'surrender' and agree that he can join the team. Aren't you?"

"Maybe.... Yes," I said, with a smile. "After all, Uncle George said I can pick the team."

Then, I stopped and faced him. "Seriously, Bob, you're not going to be happy with some of my choices."

"Some of your choices." He paused in thought for a moment, and from the change in his expression I could detect the exact instant that he realized what I was hinting at. "You don't mean...?"

"That's right. I don't have anything like a plan yet, but I think

25

I'm going to need your niece, Ginger. Don't worry, her role will be advisory and well away from the action."

"Hmmm. That's what we all thought the last time...."

3 THE INVESTIGATION BEGINS

Early November, 1980
Halifax, Nova Scotia

"How's it going?" asked Don, as we walked along the Halifax harbourfront. We didn't discuss my case when we were at Don's place for fear that it might be bugged, despite Don's periodic electronic sweeps to try to identify such things. We didn't use his phone for sensitive conversations either, for the same reason.

"Arrgh. I've gone through all the files the Admiral gave you for me, and it's like I was told. There have been serious leaks, but the only patterns in them seem to be that it was always information sold to various different parties: friends, foes, or criminals, and that they seem like crimes of opportunity. Like the Avro Arrow information all coming together at once and just when other countries were interested in getting their hands on it. Or the set of false identities all happening to become available at one time and in a single file."

"That's pretty much what the Admiral said to me when he handed me the files. How about the summaries of the investigations that were done?"

"None of the investigations turned up any clues, and in each of the cases there was enough police – military cooperation that the information could have been hijacked from either service.

"As far as the possible suspects go, every one of their background checks was gone over with a fine-tooth comb by Uncle George's and the Admiral's predecessors, and they found nothing. If any of them has been living beyond their known sources of income, taking expensive vacations, or racking up big gambling debts, then they've kept it well hidden."

"So they're all very clean or at least one of them is very, very careful," mused Don.

"Yes, but I think we could have assumed that from the start, given that whomever it is hasn't slipped up and been caught."

"Yes, that makes sense. Any other thoughts?"

"One thing that struck me after reading all the files was that there was another incident that wasn't even mentioned."

"What?"

"Yes. Remember when our government was trying to negotiate offshore mineral-rights access and secure a future strategic-mineral development, while I was running around Ottawa trying to protect Dr. MacKay's daughter from an international mercenary group that was trying to thwart us?[28]"

"Of course, that's when you got into that big shoot-out that still gives me nightmares!"

"Well, that's another time when, despite everyone's best efforts to maintain secrecy, information was getting to the bad guys that should have been nearly impossible to obtain. Information that nearly got me killed several times over. Everyone naturally suspected the Soviets in that case, with some justification I might add, but it wasn't from them that the mercenaries got their information. So who?"

"Good question, but look, whatever you do this could be the

most dangerous thing you've ever attempted."

"More dangerous than accepting your proposal of marriage?" I teased.

"Alex! This is serious," he protested.

"OK. I know."

"At a minimum, you're going to have to be on your guard and assume that the leak knows that you're on the hunt. Depending on the person and how well placed they are, they may also try to interfere, misdirect, or even come after you directly."

"I know. That's going to really complicate things. I can't trust anyone but I'll have to trust some people in order to make any progress."

"Welcome to the world of espionage. It means only trusting people as far as you have to, and always bearing in mind that whomever you're dealing with at any given time could betray you."

I shuddered. "Maybe it's time to go back to regular police work."

"You can, you know."

"I know." I sighed. "But I said I'd take this case on and now I have to see it through."

Don turned and looked into my eyes for a few moments, as if to test my resolve. Whatever he saw there must have convinced him, because he sighed in return and I knew he was resigned to it.

"What next then?" he asked.

"Next, is to check in with Bob when I'm back in Ottawa,

***

When I returned to Ottawa, one of the first things I did was to check-in at the office and ask Bob for his advice.

"You've read all the file summaries?"

"Yes. When I was in Halifax. There really didn't seem to be anything there to follow up on."

"I agree. That's what I discovered when I went through them myself."

"Can you think of anything that might have been missed, or anything I should try?"

Bob sighed. "I been thinking about that, but I don't have anything specific to suggest. There have been a whole series of people that have looked into this already: my predecessor, Uncle

George's predecessor, and the military intelligence people. Everyone has drawn a blank."

"Do you think there really is anyone to find then? Could it have been just be a series of isolated incidents over the years?"

"Possibly, but I doubt it. Maybe I've been in this game too long to believe in coincidences, but I think Uncle George and the admiral are probably right that someone has been playing games. If so, they've been very smart about it, and very careful not to overdo it."

"So what do you suggest, then?" I asked.

Bob shrugged. "Just do what Uncle George asked you to do: bring a fresh perspective, question everything, challenge our assumptions, and think outside the box. In the meantime, you'll still be getting other assignments as usual. Is there anything you need?"

"No. Not right now. Not until I get some ideas, at least."

"Well, you know where to find me if you need anything, or even if you just want to talk things over."

So that was that. Since I didn't have any 'out of the box' ideas, I decided to pursue the one incident that had affected me, and which everyone else seemed to have overlooked: the leaks that had almost gotten me killed in the Diefenbunker[29].

One of the advantages of working in K Section: Special Operations[30], was that my assignments crossed the boundaries between straightforward crimes, intelligence, and counter-intelligence. As a result, people were used to me sticking my nose into all kinds of things, and it wouldn't have seemed out of the ordinary when I signed myself into the files room of F Section: Files. First, I searched for the file on the two East German agents I had exposed and helped to catch back in 1977[31], but that was just to provide cover in case anyone did get to wondering what I'd been looking for in the files. Before I left, I would even sign the file out to add to my cover story.

Next, I went after what I was really looking for: my file, and the files on the twenty 'possibles' that had been listed for me by the Uncle George and Admiral White.

When I found the Security Service's file on me, I flipped it open and gave the contents a cursory glance. Nothing seemed amiss. I was about to move on to other files when it dawned on me that it was strange that nothing should seem amiss, so I looked over my file once more. That time it hit me. It was on the page stapled to the inside cover: the sign-out list. What was interesting was what wasn't there. No one had signed it out in the days before the Diefenbunker episode, yet someone had passed information about me to both the as-yet unidentified international criminal organization and also to Soviet intelligence. That suggested that our leak was someone working in the Ottawa sections of the Security Service, as anyone else would have had to get the file signed out just to be able to read it – either that, or our leak didn't need the file because they already had the information in their head.

Although I wasn't surprised, it was both disappointing and frightening to realize that our leak was probably within the Force rather than within military intelligence.

Next, I drew the files of the twenty possibles. Although I'd read the summaries provided by Admiral White, I was curious to see whether there was anything different in our own service's files. For the most part, the two sets of files matched well with two exceptions. One of the twenty was a fellow in the diplomatic service for whom there had been an accusation that he could be a security risk with a communist past. This person had then been subjected to exhaustive investigation by the RCMP and also by the Department of External Affairs, and had been pronounced 'safe' by both. Although the conclusion was the same in each file, the Security Service one had more details concerning the investigation. Those details, although interesting, didn't seem to leave any questions unanswered. Although the poor fellow would probably be under a shadow of suspicion forever, I didn't see anything for me to follow-up on.

The second person of interest, Staff Sergeant Avery Blunt, actually worked in the Security Service and had been suspected of having communist leanings based on his days (in the 1950s) as a university student in the United States, where one of the things he studied was Marxism. It was probably doubly unfortunate for him that his last name was the same as that of one of the members of the infamous Soviet spy ring, the Cambridge Five[32]. Blunt, for his part, had consistently denied having ever done more than study the subject in his student days and apparently no one, including the RCMP, the FBI, MI5, or MI6 had come up with any real evidence to the contrary. This I already knew from reading the corresponding file I had been given by Admiral White. I also found it hard to believe that much suspicion remained, given that S/Sgt. Blunt was now head of B Section, Counter-Intelligence.

What was not in the Admiral's file, however was a somewhat rumpled, hand-written note that read "Might be worth checking to find out why subject was placed on the FBI Index." The note was unsigned. I had heard of the FBI Index. It was basically a blacklist established by J. Edgar Hoover[33] that contained the names of people the FBI considered to be highly suspicious or worse. Given the paranoia of the times, I had the impression that it was a very long list, but my curiosity was piqued and I made a mental note to check with my friend in the FBI.

On my way out, I did sign out the file relating to the East German agents' case, just to maintain my ruse, but I didn't bother to read it. I'd written most of it myself.

My next step was to call Mary to get Uncle George to call the Deputy Director of the FBI, to get approval for Special Agent Vivian Rule to help me secretly, when asked. Vivian and I had worked on previous cases together[34,35] and were both colleagues and friends. My request was quickly accomplished, and the next day found me using a downtown, public pay-phone to call her at her office.

"What's up Alex? The Deputy Director says to give you whatever help you need. You're not on a mole-hunt, are you?"

"It's a bit more complicated than that, but essentially, yes."

"Jeez. I was only kidding.... OK. What do you need."

"For now, just information. Is the FBI Index still active?"

"Sure. We don't call it that any more, but all the old files have been retained."

"Can you check a name for me: Avery Blunt. He's a Staff Sergeant in the Security Service, and I'm interested in anything you might have on him, including why you might have a record of him at all. Also, can you check for a file on him without anyone knowing about it?"

"Whew. You don't ask for much, do you?"

"Sorry. If it makes you feel any better, I just pulled the same kind of stunt with our own administration section."

"OK. Leave it with me. Where are you anyway? I can hear the sounds of vehicles going by."

"I'm calling from a pay phone. My phones might be bugged."

"Even your office!" Vivian exclaimed. Then, more thoughtfully, "you think your mole, or leak, or whatever might be well enough placed to be aware of your assignment."

It was a statement, rather than a question, but I answered it anyway. "Yes. I'm assuming so anyway. If you want to reach me at home or in the office, ask for Cathy or leave a message for Cathy if you get an answering machine. I'll phone you back when I can."

"Who's Cathy?"

"I don't know. It's just the first name that popped into my head."

"OK. Cloak and dagger stuff! Sounds like fun."

"Maybe, but watch out for daggers heading for you. I'm probably going to upset more than a few people before I'm done."

The next day, I received a call on my office phone. A muffled, man's voice asked to speak to Cathy, and when I said they had the wrong number the man swore rather graphically and hung up. It took me twenty minutes to leave the office and drive to a suitable public pay-phone to call Vivian in her office.

"Who was it that made the phone call for you?" I asked when Vivian came on the line.

She chuckled. "I asked a colleague here in the office to do it, not to ask any questions, and not to sound like an FBI agent. Here's what I found out. There is a file on your person of interest, but there's not much in it. The file was started back in '50s because in his student days he took a university course in Marxism down here."

"And?"

"And it was given a cursory check, but he didn't actually join any of the Marxist, communist, or fascist movements, and it seemed that he didn't even participate in any of the campus rallies. So, his file was simply retained as a possible person of interest in case other information came to light later."

"But nothing did?"

"Not much. There are several notes on the file that show when requests for information on him were received from your Security Service and MI6. That's the kind of thing that can make people suspicious, but the requests could have been simply part of Canadian or NATO checks for security clearances…. There is one other thing though. There is an old-looking, hand-written note stapled to the inside cover of his file saying 'Could be Gideon,' with a large question mark."

"Gideon. A cryptonym[36]?"

"Yes. We have an index file for cryptonyms, so I looked it up. The name Gideon has been used quite a few times over the years to refer to people or projects. Assuming that in this case the reference is to a person then there are still quite a few references, but only one to someone operating in Canada."

"Yes?"

"In 1959, someone contacted the U.S. Air Force offering to sell us classified information on the Avro Arrow jet fighter you people had developed. His code name was Gideon. The Air Force person contacted us to see whether we were familiar with the name, but we weren't. In the end, the Air Force decided that they already knew as much about the project as they needed to, so the contact wasn't pursued and the matter was dropped. The name Gideon was flagged though, in case it ever came up again."

"Thanks Vivian. I'll keep digging on my end."

After thinking about it a bit, I decided to keep the name Gideon to myself for a while, rather than run around asking whether anyone recognized it. Even at the time, I realized that I was becoming paranoid, but I didn't know how best to proceed and decided to keep as low a profile as possible until I knew more.

The next time I entered Bob's office, he said "I can tell from the look in your eyes that you have questions."

"Always," I said with a laugh. "In this case I have a few. Do we keep a master list of cryptonyms?"

"Like the FBI does? No, but we probably should. I have one of my own, and I'm positive that the heads of A and B Ops[37] each have their own."

"And do they share with each other?"

Bob chuckled. "Officially, yes, but probably not. It all depends on the circumstances and the personalities of the people involved at any given time."

"Need to know only?"

"Always. But beyond that, there are some things that the heads would probably keep to them selves even in the face of a direct order from the Commissioner himself. What are you after?"

"Well, I was wondering how readily accessible such information would be, and I'm also interested in the cryptonym Gideon."

"Gideon." Bob's eyes lit up. "Go ahead and ask the heads about it if you want. Use Uncle George's name if you have to, but I can tell you a little bit about it myself because I also came across it when I was walking in your boots.

"In the Avro Arrow incident, someone got hold of everything needed to build the Arrow. I mean everything: blueprints, parts lists, assembly instructions, manuals… everything, and then tried quietly shopping them around. He approached the British and the Americans for sure; possibly also the French. We got wind of this through the British, who said that he identified himself as Gideon. From the FBI, we learned that Gideon made the same offer to the USAF."

"And he really did sell to the British."

"Right. So much had already been shared between the RCAF and the USAF that the Americans didn't need to buy anything, and as far as anyone knows the French didn't pursue the matter at all."

"Did the name Gideon ever turn up again?"

"A few times, over the years, but only as speculation. It became kind of a joke after a while. People would say 'maybe it was Gideon' meaning that they really had no idea."

For the next few weeks, I worked on other cases while I waited for inspiration or opportunity. I got the latter, one day, when Bob mentioned that there was going to be a two-day information sharing conference involving the heads of all of the RCMP and military intelligence sections. The idea was to pool information and to make sure that the 'left hand' knew what the 'right hand' was doing, as the old saying went. The first day of the two-day conference would involve briefings on the domestic intelligence situation, while the second day would have briefings on the international intelligence situation. Since the sessions were open to anyone with Top Secret, or better, security clearance, I simply had to sign-up to get in as an observer. For me, this would be an opportunity to put faces to the names of the people on the watch-list that Admiral White had given me because I had only previously met some of them.

The conference was held in a secure meeting room in our headquarters building and comprised about 45 people, including all of the 20 that I was interested in, and I already knew about half of the 20. I focused about half of my attention on the intelligence briefings, particularly the ones on international security since I hadn't had much exposure to that side of the business. I was well acquainted with our close relationship with the FBI, since I'd worked with them myself several times, but was interested to see how closely we worked with the intelligence community of the rest of the Five Eyes[38] nations.

I focused the other half of my attention on the 'people of interest,' particularly those that I had not previously met. In this area, there were no startling revelations, of course, but I did come away with first impressions and a better feeling for what everyone looked like than I'd been able to gather from mere photographs. That made me feel a bit better, for some reason, possibly because unknown demons are scarier than known ones.

Two people whose personalities did stand out somewhat seemed, at first glance, to be polar opposites. Staff Sergeant Avery Blunt, whose name had come to my attention through our files, as well as those of the FBI, came across as one of the nicest people you'd ever want to meet. I had to remind myself that dark things could lurk under the guise of an outwardly friendly manner. The other one, Staff Sergeant Alexander Demeniak, who was the head of A Section, Security Screening, came across as cranky, narrow-minded, and one of the fossils, as I thought of them, that regularly let it be known that there was no place in policing or the military for women. For him, I had to remind myself that he wasn't necessarily guilty just because I didn't like him or his mannerisms. Unfortunately, since one was the head of counter-intelligence and the other security screening, I was going to have to talk to each of them.

I didn't think the technical side of the event advanced my case at first, but in subsequent days an idea began to percolate. One of the presenters at the conference had discussed attempts – thus far unsuccessful – to identify an arms dealer that was operating in Canada and was somehow able to gain access to Canadian Forces weapons. That gave me the idea for a sting operation in which it might be possible to tempt our leak into action and at least show how the information flowed. This too, I kept to myself until an opportunity arose.

My next steps were going to be trying to meet with each of the 'possibles.' This took some time to arrange, and required a cover story. After talking it over with Bob, we arranged that he would 'assign' me to work on an old, unresolved case from 1959. It wasn't a particularly important case, but it had the virtues of being real, dating from the same time period as the Avro Arrow incidents, and unimportant and non-threatening enough to amuse people with the fact that I'd been stuck with such a dead-end task. "If people jump to the conclusion that you're being punished for something," commented Bob, "then so much the better. They might let something slip."

I won't go through the details of each of my meetings with these people, except to summarize those with Staff Sergeants Blunt and Demeniak.

Staff Sergeant Blunt was friendly and accommodating, insisting that I call him by his first name, but he was nobody's fool and immediately dismissed my cover story.

"That case is dead and cold, where it belongs. What are you really after?" he asked.

That shook me, so I admitted that he was right and that I really had been assigned to look into an old case that dated back to 1959, but that my orders came from the Deputy Commissioner, and I couldn't tell him what it really was.

"OK," he said, leaning back in his chair. "That makes a bit more sense. How can I help?"

"Can you tell me what cases stand out in your memory from that time?" I asked.

He thought in silence for a few moments. "Well, in 1958 there was a nuclear reactor incident at Chalk River[39]. This had been the second significant nuclear accident at Chalk River and we were called in to assess security measures and make recommendations.

"Then there was the Gouzenko affair[40] of course. The Royal Commission brought a bunch of things to the surface that we had to chase down, not to mention things that came up during the various trials. All together that kept us pretty busy until at least 1962."

"Was there ever any indication there might have been leaks in the security or intelligence communities?" I asked.

"Ah ha," he pounded. "So that's what you're really after is it?"

"Look," I tried again. "I'm sorry, but I'm not allowed to tell you anything specific. Not yet, at least."

"Fine." He smiled. Genuinely, I thought. "Ask your questions and I'll answer as best I can. No, there were no indications or accusations of leaks from the intelligence community. There were some university professors, some scientists from the National Research Council, a few people from the Department of Munitions and Supply, and some low-level administrative people in places like External Affairs, the Bureau of Statistics, the Bank of Canada, and even the National Film Board."

"External Affairs?" I asked.

"Yes, a cipher clerk, I think. I don't remember the name, but it will be in the files."

I made a note to follow that one up.

"Anything else?"

"Well, the only other big deal was the cancellation of the Avro Arrow program."

"And?" I prompted.

"Well, we were involved in helping to round up all the secret material: files, reports, and drawings - that sort of thing – and make sure they were all destroyed."

"And were they?" I tried to keep my face blank and my voice neutral.

"No. Now that you mention it, some of the material was either not handed over or diverted away from destruction. It was quite embarrassing for everyone at the time, because the British actually contacted us to tell us that someone had offered to sell them a complete set of plans, drawings and manuals for the Arrow, and that they had gone ahead and bought them."

"What happened?"

"Well, the British returned everything to us of course. They even said they'd tried to discover who the source was but failed. It was damn embarrassing I can tell you. It made us look like fools regardless of whether it was a leak, a mole, or just plain incompetence somewhere along the line.

"If you dig hard enough, you'll discover I was peripherally involved, so I'll just tell you straight out. I was a young Corporal at the time, helping shred Arrow documents. It was tedious work, but when the dam burst all of us went from boredom to panic in a hurry! We were all afraid we'd be fired even if we hadn't done anything wrong."

"Had you?"

"You're very direct."

"I'm not dumb enough to play games with the head of counter-intelligence, and I'm no psychologist," I responded.

"From what I hear, you're not dumb at all, and you don't have to be a psychologist as long as you have your dog with you." He looked pointedly at Silver, who was lying on the floor beside my chair, watching everything.

"What have you heard?"

"About you? That you're the Director's rising star. About your dog? People are saying you think he's part psychic."

"And that I'm crazy?"

"No, I haven't heard that," he chuckled. "But you'd be smart to assume people think it."

"Why do I get the feeling that you don't?" I asked.

"I've read your case files, and Bob's notes on them. The people you've put away seem to be absolutely convinced that you and your dog are both part psychic. For myself, I don't believe in that kind of stuff, but one way or the other you always seem to get the job done and that's what counts the most around here."

"So, if I asked what you know about Gideon, you'd tell me the truth?"

"With him watching me with that intent stare of his?" He looked at Silver again. "No. Normally, I'd tell you nothing at all, but in this case, I'll make an exception because I want Gideon caught too."

I raised an eyebrow.

"No, it isn't me, but I don't expect you to take my word for it. In fact, I know that there's still a shadow over a bunch of us old-timers because Gideon was never identified and it could be any of us. I also know that the FBI suspected me, and probably still does, although they have a tendency to suspect everyone of everything anyway. Naturally, I'd like to get my name cleared, but I tried to find out who Gideon is, or was, and failed, so if you can do it, you'll have my blessing, and my thanks too."

"Do you know who it was on the British side that raised the alert? I read the file, but couldn't find it."

"That's because it isn't there to find. He was basically a source trying to help us out so, to protect him, his name was never mentioned; never written down.'

"But you know who it was?"

"I know who it had to have been." He paused and stared at me for a while, then seemed to make a decision. "Don't write this down, but the name you want is Major Jack Evans. In 1959, he was the Defence Attaché, at the British High Commission here in Ottawa. I don't know whether he's still in the service, or even if he's still alive."

"I think I'll go see if I can find out. Thank you for your help, I really appreciate it," I said as I stood up to leave.

"Just do me two favours: find the bastard for us, and always remember that if anyone asked, I told you…."

"Nothing. You told me nothing at all."

He nodded in appreciation as we left.

Meeting with Staff Sergeant Demeniak, the head of A Section, Security Screening, was completely different. In the first place he refused to see me at all, claiming that he was too busy. When I got Bob to go to bat for me Demeniak gave him exactly the same treatment. Bob didn't take that lightly and got the Deputy Commissioner to call him, after which Demeniak ungraciously consented to "spare me a few minutes."

Unsurprisingly, he was hostile, vulgar, and sexist in his comments. This produced a low warning growl from Silver that actually prompted him to tell me to "get that dog" out of his office before he shot him. I was in full tactical uniform at the time, as we had just returned from a call, and when I stood up, I could see in his eyes when it dawned on him that I was armed and he wasn't. Not that he'd have shot Silver anyway, of course, nor I him, but it did put him on the defensive for the first time.

For my part, I avoided calling him an asshole to his face – barely – and simply smiled sweetly, said "Thank you Staff," and left. "Smile," a sergeant had once advised me. "It makes people wonder what you're up to." I've always liked that one and have used it a few times to good effect.

I continued smiling as I walked down the corridor, but my teeth were grating and my jaw was clenched. Even Silver looked up at me from time to time trying to judge my mood.

So, I hadn't learned anything useful from Staff Sergeant Demeniak and, in the end, I didn't learn much I didn't already know from any of the others I interviewed, whether they were in the RCMP, Department of External Affairs, or the military. Some of the latter I'd had to travel to Halifax to see, and it was in Halifax that I got wind of another opportunity. Strangely enough, it came from a news report I heard on the radio.

Laurie Schramm

4 A SECRET MEETING

January 22, 1981
Halifax, NS.

"Don, would you take me to a hockey game?" I asked as Don, Silver, and I were walking along the Halifax harbourfront.

Although it sounds un-Canadian to say it, I wasn't a huge hockey fan but I knew that Don was. So, in the pause that followed, I imagined him doing a mental double-take.

"Uh, sure," he said. "Did you have a particular game in mind?"

"Actually, I do. On the news today I heard that after postponing it twice[41], they've finally settled on a schedule for the Canada Cup and I want to see one of the games." This much anticipated hockey tournament was finally going to get underway between teams from the six 'best hockey countries' in the world: Canada, Soviet Union, United States, Sweden, Czechoslovakia, and Finland. Games and the various rounds were going to be held at arenas in Edmonton, Winnipeg, Montreal and Ottawa.

"Any particular reason for this sudden interest in hockey?"

"Well, it's the talk of the town. Around the office, everyone seems to think that the series will come down to Canada against either the Soviets or the Americans."

"Probably. What game do you want to see?"

"I want to see the championship final between Canada and the Soviets. It's going to be on September 13 at the Montreal Forum[42]."

"What makes you so sure those will be the two finalists? Anything can happen in a hockey tournament, you know. Unexpected injuries, even, can make a big difference."

"Yes, I know. I guess I'm playing the odds. Maybe we should get tickets for the two semi-final games as well, just in case. Besides, I think I should learn more about our national game and this is in the nature of *homework*."

I didn't place heavy emphasis on the last word, but we had arranged to use a code word for my mission in the course of our personal conversations: homework.

Don picked up on our codeword and stopped probing.

"OK. Let me see what I can do."

"Thanks. I'll try from my end too, but it will improve our odds if we both try."

"Sounds good to me."

My next call was to Mary MacLeod, the Deputy Commissioner's wife.

"Mary, this is Alex Houston. We met at your husband's promotion party at your house."

"I remember it well Alex, how are you?"

"Just fine, thank you. I have a special request, but it's going to sound frivolous."

"I'm sure it will be fine dear. What is it you need?"

"I'd like to get two tickets for each of the semi-final games and also for the final game of the Canada Cup hockey tournament. The final's going to be at the Montreal Forum on September 13th."

"You want to go to three hockey games?"

"Well, not really, but I think there's going to be someone at one or two of them that I'd like to have a quiet talk with. Someone that I don't want anyone to know I'm speaking to. Not even Bob."

"All right dear. I understand. I'll talk to George about it, but I don't know whether he can help or not, I heard on the news that all of those games are selling out fast."

"I know, that's why I'm asking for help. If it helps, I don't need good seats, I just need a pair of seats anywhere in the building, even if it's in the nosebleeds[43]."

"Give us a few days and then call me back."

Thanking her, I said goodbye and hung up. Now, I just had to wait and hope for two lucky breaks: one that I could get tickets, and the other that the Soviet team would actually make it to one of the final games.

Once again, it was hurry-up and wait. I never liked the waiting part but, with me back in Ottawa, my regular duties kept me busy with routine things until the fall, and I did do a few things related to what I now thought of as my Gideon Case. One of the latter that later turned out to be important was tracking down the British Military Attaché from the Avro Arrow incident.

Don and I spent so much time apart that we normally had a nightly phone chat no matter where our respective jobs took us. I have already mentioned our choosing a personal code word for my mission (homework). We'd also come up with a list of places that had a public pay phone Don could go to if I ever said that I'd like to discuss my 'homework' with him sometime. In such a case, he would go to the next place on the list, and I would call him there from a randomly chosen pay phone wherever I was. In this way, we'd never use the same phone combination twice. I kept my copy of the list in a hidden compartment in Silver's collar.

The first place on the list was just outside the Dartmouth fast-food restaurant in which Don and I had first met. When I phoned Don there, it was to ask him to quietly see if he could find out what had happened to the Major Jack Evans that had been Defence Attaché at the British High Commission in 1959 when Gideon had made contact about selling the Avro Arrow plans.

Several days later, a call to my office phone yielded a muffled male voice asking for Cathy. When I explained that he must have dialed the wrong number, the voice said: "Are you sure? It's pretty important I talk to her. It's about her homework." I repeated "Sorry, but you must have dialed the wrong number." The voice then grumbled something I couldn't make out and hung up.

Reaching for Silver's collar, I removed it to access the second list I had hidden there. This one had a list of Ottawa pay-phone locations at which Don could call me. Silver and I left the office to drive to the next unused one on my list.

I was starting to feel conspicuous loitering around public pay-phones by this time, so I was relieved when this latest one began to ring. It was Don, of course, and he had the information I'd asked for.

"It's Colonel Jack Evans now, but retired. He's now a widower, and living in England."

"Do you have an address for him?"

"An address but no phone. It's in Bath."

"Hmmm. I suppose it doesn't matter. He'd hardly be willing to talk to a stranger on the phone about intelligence matters. Even ancient ones. I may need to go pay him a visit. We'll see."

While we had each other on the phone, we chatted about a few other things, but they weren't related to the case. My first instinct turned out to be right though: I was going to have to go look him up later on.

***

Early September, 1981

"Have you been watching the series?" Bob asked me one day when we ran into each other at the office coffee machine. He didn't need to identify what he meant by 'series,' almost everyone in Canada had been watching the hockey series and it was the main topic of conversation in coffee shops across the country, even to the point of beating-out Canadians' favourite topic: the weather.

"A bit. Mostly on TV. I saw Canada beat Finland during the first round, and I watched Canada beat the Americans in the second round. I missed the third and fourth round games, but Don and I actually got to go to the semi-final game here in town and watched the Soviets beat the Czechs 4 - 1."

"Lucky you. Are you going in on the office pool for the final game?"

"You bet." I didn't tell him, or anyone, that I'd gotten my real wish already: the final game was going to be between Canada and the Soviets, and Don and I had tickets for the game, which would be at the Montreal Forum.

September 13, 1981
Montreal, QC

Don and I flew to Montreal and, since I was on duty, I was able to bring Silver on the plane with us. When we arrived at the Montreal Airport on the morning of game day, we were met outside the terminal building by an unremarkable-looking sedan.

When the driver got out to help us with our luggage, my first impression was that he looked like he could have been a defensive lineman for a professional football team: large, well muscled, but with a spring in his step that suggested remarkable agility. A second glance revealed that I had met him before on an earlier case[44]. Silver, of course, had recognized him right away and didn't react to him at all.

"Sergeant Wilson!" I exclaimed. "The last time we met you were in full battledress, armed to the teeth, and bundling me into a 5-ton army truck."

He gave me a huge smile. "I'm surprised that you remember me Ma'am, and I'm sure glad you survived that one. The scuttlebutt is that you did some real damage with that shotgun you were carrying."

"Well, I was very lucky and I feel fortunate to have been able to walk away more or less intact, Sergeant."

"Frank Ma'am – remember?"

"Only if you call me Alex – remember?"

"Fair enough," he said, chuckling as he helped us load our bags and get in.

As we drove away, I noticed that we didn't have to tell him where we were staying. Don had obviously given him the address already.

When we had travelled the main highway from the airport and exited into the downtown core, I glanced behind us from time to time and was just about to make a comment when I noticed Frank looking at me in the rear-view mirror.

"Don't worry Ma'am... I mean Alex, that car following us is one of ours."

"Do you remember meeting Lieutenant Sandy Moore a few years ago[45]?" asked Don.

"The helicopter pilot? Yes, he picked me up in Alaska, flying one of those giant helicopters of yours."

"Well, that's him back there. He's following us to make sure no one else does, if you know what I mean."

"I do, but what's a helicopter pilot from the Pacific Fleet doing driving a car here?"

"Well, Sandy works for us. He's a very capable fellow, just like Sergeant Wilson here. You'd be amazed at some of the things they can do, but their most important qualification right now is that I'd trust them with my life – and yours."

It seems that no one else was following us so, without the need for evasive maneuvers, we were efficiently deposited at our hotel, where we checked into a very nice suite – using false names and addresses. Don even had a credit card and an Ontario driver's licence made out in the false name he was using.

We had arrived in time for lunch and a nice walk around town with Silver, and hadn't been back in our suite long before there was a knock on the door. When I went to open the door, there was a loud squeal of delight.

"Alex!" said Ginger Brandt, the famous Canadian TV and film actress. We had met several years earlier when she helped me with a case[46], at the suggestion of her uncle, who was also my boss, Bob.

"Ginger! It's been too long." We exchanged a longish and heartfelt hug, after which I led her into the room. "Don, come see who's here." Don came in from the other room, but Silver beat him to Ginger, having rushed up and stood on his two back legs so he could get a few licks in.

Don had to look at her quite intently before he realized who she was. "Ginger!" he exclaimed. "But you don't look like Ginger Brandt."

"Elizabeth Peterson is my real name," she corrected. "Ginger Brandt is my stage name, and this" – she pointed to herself with a sweeping motion – "is the disguise I use when I want to get away from my fans and the media." As she stood there in our suite, she appeared to be two or three inches shorter than Ginger the actress (who wore high heels), had hazel-coloured eyes (instead of Ginger's blue contact lenses), lustrous, medium-brown hair cut short (instead of Ginger's long blond wig), wore no makeup (which Ginger would never do), and had glasses (which Ginger didn't). I'd seen her dress like this before, but the effect was still remarkable. The one thing she couldn't hide was her brilliant smile.

"I still can't get over how effortlessly you pull this off," I said.

"Well, I'm an actress, so it's kind of like another role. Besides, I do it so often that I can switch personalities almost without thinking, and it does me good to spend some time as the real me every once in a while."

After catching up a bit on things since we'd last seen each other, Ginger brought our meeting to order, saying: "All right Alex. What are you really up to?"

"As you know, the big hockey game is tonight. The Soviets are going to have two big things on their minds: winning the game and, more importantly, making sure none of their players try to defect after the game. Because of that, their intelligence people are going to be watching everything and everybody very closely. I want to have a quiet chat with one of those intelligence people."

"Are you sure the person you want will be there?"

"Not for sure, no. But he's pretty senior over there, and I think they'll have everyone out in full force. In any case, it's a chance I have to take, but I don't want their watchers to recognize me if they see me talking to him. That's where you come in. Did you bring everything?"

"You bet," she said, lifting the medium-sized suitcase she was carrying. "Are you ready to get started?"

'Yes," I said, excitedly.

"OK then. Don, if you wouldn't mind taking Silver for a long walk, we have some things to do. Give us at least 45 minutes and then come back. You'll be the judge and jury."

When Don and Silver had left, Ginger got down to business. Opening her suitcase, she first removed two cases. One was a makeup case and the other contained a blond wig.

"Is that one of yours?" I asked. "Sure is," she replied. "I have a room full of duplicates so we can switch them out as fast as they get damaged or worn out, but let's start with makeup."

"But I don't wear makeup and, anyway, I only need to look different from a distance. I don't expect to get very close to any of the watchers, just the man I want to talk to."

"The makeup isn't so much a part of the physical disguise. It's to help make you feel the new look. The more you feel different, the more your body language will fit the disguise rather than the real you. Trust me, OK?"

"You know I do."

"Good. Then sit down and relax. This is going to be fun."

So, I tried to suffer in silence while Ginger gave me the full treatment: lotions, powders, eyebrow pencil, mascara, false eyelashes, the works. So much so, that I fully expected to look quite garish, but when she had me look into a mirror, I was astonished to see that everything had been done very subtly. It was me, but it wasn't me.

"Amazing," I exclaimed. "After all that work, you've only

changed everything a little bit, but it changed everything."

"Exactly. If I paint you up like an actor on stage and give you monstrous eyelashes, it would produce exactly the wrong effect. We're not trying to make your *face* stand out, we're just trying to make it difficult to recognize."

Something about the way she said the word face caught my attention, and she noticed.

"Yes. We will be a little more drastic with some other parts of you, beginning with these. Since you aren't used to wearing contact lenses, we'll use glasses." She then had me try on several pairs of glasses (with plain glass lenses) before deciding on one. "And now the hair." She had actually brought two blond wigs with her, and had me model each before deciding on one. Then she brought up the mirror again. "Look" she said, expectantly.

I gasped, then giggled. "I can't believe it!"

"Neither will Don, but we aren't finished yet. Let's try some clothes. I'd like to put you in high heels to change your height but, since you aren't used to them, you'll just wobble around and be lucky not to fall over and draw attention to yourself – the wrong kind of attention. So, once again, we're going to be a bit more subtle. A nice top and skirt that you can wear with the shoes you already have on."

"Ugh. Do I have to wear a skirt?"

"Let's not go through that again. I want you to do almost everything except what you usually do. That means almost nothing you're comfortable with. Right?"

"Fine," I grumbled. I wasn't looking forward to this as much any more.

"My goodness," she said, "trying to get you looking feminine is like trying to get Silver to go near water. Now, suck it up and try these on."

Once again, she had brough a couple of skirts and a couple of tops. The skirts were short – not miniskirts, but close, and the tops were more revealing than anything I was used to wearing. After modelling every possible combination for her, Ginger selected one. She certainly had a good eye and a good memory, as everything fitted me quite well.

"Not bad," she decided. "Now try the top with one of these." She reached into her suitcase and brought out a couple of bras.

"But I already have... push-up bras? Oh no. That's going too far."

"Humour me," she said. "See which one fits best. It needs to be comfortable or you'll be fidgeting and readjusting everything all the time."

So, I clamped my jaw and tried those on too. Surprisingly, I found one that wasn't anywhere near as uncomfortable to wear as it looked.

"OK, now one more thing." Out from her suitcase came pantyhose, quite sheer and natural in colour, but in slightly different shades. Now that my outfit had been selected, she picked one out right away, saying: "These should do nicely. Just enough colour to warm-up your pale skin."

Once I had everything on, Ginger made me practice walking around the suite until I relaxed a bit, then said: "Fine. Let's go down to the lobby. We'll surprise Don when he and Silver walk in and see what he thinks."

"OK. Wait a minute." I felt around the top of the skirt. "There aren't any pockets. Where am I going to put everything?"

"Ah yes, I thought of that." Back in to her suitcase she went and brought out a small, tan-coloured leather purse that would go with almost anything casual. "I thought you might feel undressed without that little derringer of yours," she said, handing it over.

Sure enough, there was just enough room for my wallet, a few tissues, and the fancy-looking, double-barreled silver derringer that I often wore concealed when I was working undercover. "It looks like a toy, doesn't it? But it takes .38 Special rounds and is deadly at close range."

Ginger looked at it, shuddered, and said "Let's go."

A few minutes later, we were in the hotel lobby where we found a couple of comfortable chairs with a good view of the main entrance. Not too comfortable however, as I couldn't just flop down in the softest looking easy chair like I would have with pants on. While we waited, Ginger and I continued to catch up on things, trading stories of some of my recent cases for her accounts of recent film sets, TV episodes, and a new movie she was going to be filming soon. Before I knew it, there were Don and Silver coming in the front door.

"Don! Over here!" Ginger called out, with a wave.

Silver immediately spotted us and led Don to where we were

sitting. As he approached, I stood up and watched as he spotted me, looked me up and down with a quizzical expression on his face. Then he looked at me again and did a gratifying double-take. "Alex!?" It was half exclamation, half question.

"That's me. Same old Alex," I replied, with a wink.

"It's amazing," said Don. "I would have walked right past you. It's only up close that your face and your green eyes give you away."

"Yes, well almost no one is going to get that close, and its not her eyes they're going to be looking at, is it?"

"I'll say," said Don, looking me up and down again.

"Don!!" I exclaimed, and he had the grace to blush. Very cute.

"So, does she pass?" asked Ginger, with a complacent smile on her face.

"She passes all right. I think she'll fool everyone except Silver."

So, now we had the disguise; we just had to wait for game time and see if it was all going to be worthwhile. When it was time to walk to the Montreal Forum, which was less than a kilometre from our hotel, I wasn't shocked to spot two men walking about a block behind us.

"A bit of an unusual looking pair wouldn't you say?' I asked Don. Sergeant Wilson, as I've already mentioned looked like he could have been a linebacker from the Montreal Alouettes, his muscles straining the fabric of his civilian clothes. He was dark-haired, and exuded a sense of rough toughness. Lieutenant Sandy Moore, in contrast, was fair-haired, a bit taller, and much thinner. He looked more like a cowboy in street clothes.

"Just a couple of friends taking in a hockey game," said Don.

"They have seats too?" I asked, surprised.

"They do. In fact, they'll be sitting almost directly behind us, but a few rows back."

"I'm amazed. How did you pull off getting an extra two seats? I can still hardly believe that Uncle George even got seats for us."

"Miracle workers. That's us. You make a wish; we'll try to make it happen."

"I wonder whether Admiral White fully appreciates the kind of talent he has on his team."

"That's what we think. Maybe you should tell him some time."

"I will, but he may think I'm just a tiny bit biased."

Our walk to the Forum was uneventful. Apparently, we weren't followed. So, all seemed well as we went in and found our seats. It was a sellout crowd of over 17,000 people. They were excited but quiet. It was almost as if the crowd was holding its collective breath.

"You still think he'll be here?" Don asked quietly, with his mouth close to my ear.

He knew in advance, of course, but Ginger didn't know, that the point of this whole exercise was that I wanted to meet 'the enemy.' Although the Soviet Union was normally the arch foe of the Western Allies, especially when it came to international intelligence work, there were times when we worked as allies again, almost like we were back in the days of the Second World War. There weren't many such times, to be sure, but one of them intersected with a case I'd fallen into in which we had a common enemy and the Soviets had contributed the services of a man named Emi, who was really an intelligence officer of their Foreign Intelligence Service (as distinct from the KGB or the GRU).

Without Emi's help I really doubt that we could have resolved the case, nor that I would have survived[47] and, as it turned out, we worked well together and became respectful colleagues even though we worked for opposing governments. At that time, he'd been Captain Emilis (Emi) Matulis and, officially, an Assistant Military Attaché at the Embassy of the Soviet Union in Ottawa. Since then, he'd been promoted to Major and made Chief Military Attaché at the embassy.

To Don's question, I replied: "After last year's defections of the Šťastný brothers from the Czechoslovakian team[48], I'll bet every intelligence officer they have will be here watching to make sure there are no Soviet defections. I'm pretty sure he'll be here too."

Although we didn't have terrific seats by hockey-fan standards, they suited my purpose admirably. We were about two-thirds of the way up the stands, but almost in line with the centre-line, and we were directly across the rink from the players' benches. I had brought a compact pair of binoculars with me – not an uncommon sight in the higher-up seats, and was using it to scan the seats on the other side, looking for Emi.

This was the most stressful part of the evening for me. I had gambled that the Soviet team would be in the series final and doubled-down by gambling that Emi would be in the crowd as part of the Soviets security force. I think Don was aware of the exact moment I spotted Emi as, with a whoosh, I released the breath I hadn't realized I was holding.

"See something?" asked Don, as nonchalantly.

"Directly behind the Soviet team's bench, about ten rows up."

"So, you can relax and watch the game now."

That made me laugh. "As I look around, I don't think there's a relaxed person in this whole building." I'd been to an NHL game in the Montreal Forum in the early 1970s, and compared with that experience the Montreal Forum was strangely quiet. Perhaps it was because so much national pride was riding on this one last game, but it was the players that were really under pressure. The Soviet team had entered the tournament as the favourite, with a mixture of seasoned and younger players and was led by the famous 'KLM Line' of Vladimir Krutov, Igor Larionov, and Sergei Makarov. The Canadian team, in comparison, was much younger, although it boasted such rising young stars as Wayne Gretzky and Ray Bourque. Both teams had done extremely well during the earlier rounds, and now they would face off against each other for the final, big game.

The first period was a nail-biter, with Canada on the offensive throughout the entire period but unable to get the puck past the Soviet's star goaltender Vladislav Tretiak. As the period ended with the score tied 0 – 0, Don and I, like almost everyone else in the arena, found ourselves sitting on the edges of our seats, still holding our breath.

"Wow," said Don. "I think it's going to be a close one. Either that, or the first goal for either side will trigger a shoot-out."

"A shoot-out, I think," I replied. "There's so much talent and energy out there, just waiting to be released."

During the first intermission, Emi seemed content to remain in his seat, so I did the same while Don went to secure some hot dogs and pop for us.

It was the Soviet team that dominated the second period, scoring a goal within the first five minutes. Although Canada quickly scored to even the score, the Soviets responded in kind with another goal to retake the lead. At that point I got up to make the long walk around to the other side of the Forum. When I got there, I stood at one of the two nearest doorways to Emi's section, to keep watch to see whether he would get up to find either a restroom or refreshments. I'd no sooner arrived at my vantage point than the crowd gave out a huge, collective groan as the Soviet team scored a power-play goal, giving them a 3 – 1 lead. Although there were still a few minutes left in the period, I saw Emi rise up from his seat and make his way to the other side of his section from the side I was on. As he did so, I quickly moved to the door on the far side of his section and waited for him to make his way up the steps.

Noticing that he seemed to be headed for one of the concession windows, I came up from behind him and said, "Buy you a hot dog, Comrade Major?"

He was too experienced to show any sign of being startled, and without breaking stride he simply said "I know that voice, and yes, I do like your decadent hot dogs."

After another couple of paces, he causally glanced at me and I saw his eyes widen as he took in my appearance.

"You're changed your hair colour since I saw you last, and grown it longer too."

"All the better to not be recognized speaking to you," I replied.

"Ah ha," he responded. "I would have had a difficult time believing that meeting you here was pure coincidence."

"No. I took a chance, hoping you'd be here helping ensure there are no embarrassing defections."

"Quite correct. A distasteful, but unavoidable assignment, I am afraid."

"May I have a brief word with you after we get our hot dogs?"

"Of course, but only if they are, as you say, 'on me' tonight."

Once we'd obtained our hot dogs, we moved to one of the many places where fans could stand and chat while eating and drinking, before returning to their seats. I congratulated him on his promotion to Major, for which he thanked me, then, after a moment he stopped talking and just looked at me, expectantly. That was my cue.

"You remember when you penetrated what we call the Diefenbunker to help me in the underwater minerals case?"

"Of course. It was not an experience easily forgotten."

"Well among all the other strange aspects of the case were the fact that you somehow knew where I would be, and you seemed to know all about me, some of my earlier cases, and Silver, too, for that matter. Much more than anyone should ever have been able to find out."

"Yes. I was hoping you'd overlook that given the other pressures we faced."

"You're half right. I noticed and chose to overlook it. I meant to ask you about it later, but the right time never seemed to materialize and I was so grateful for your help that I didn't pursue it."

"Something is telling me that you intend to pursue it now though. No?"

"Yes, because now I have a 'need to know,' as we say. I realize that if you have a mole in the Security Service or our Military Intelligence that you're not going to admit it, but I'm hoping that if you got your information from some kind of leak or information broker that you might be able to throw me a bone... Excuse me, I mean give me some kind of lead."

"Yes, I understand your 'throw me a bone,' although from where you get these strange expressions I cannot imagine. As to your question...." He paused, as if searching his memory. "I will tell you frankly that my service has no mole in your system, however I cannot speak for the KGB or the GRU. In the case where we worked together, it was much simpler. We had an intermediary – a broker, if you will – that had a source that could gain access to your service's files."

"OK. I won't ask you who your intermediary is, or was, but can you tell me anything about the source?"

He looked at me intently for a few moments, then took a bit of his hot dog – probably to buy more time – and for an instant, I didn't think he was going to say anything more. But then he did.

"You wouldn't approach me in public and ask me this unless it was very important." It was a statement, but I answered it anyway.

"Very important, and what I'm after is purely defensive, no threat to your country."

"Hmmm. Well then, for the sake of our former comradeship-in-arms together I will tell you the only things I have ever learned about this so-called source in Ottawa. First, my interpretation is that this is no ideological traitor but most likely a highly-placed opportunist motived by money and perhaps even 'the game' as our business is sometimes termed. Such people are completely untrustworthy, but can be useful if handled carefully. Secondly, the person's name – man or woman I don't know – appears to be Gideon. I am not certain of it, you understand, but I believe it is likely to be the case.... I see that the name is not unknown to you."

"No, the name is not unknown to me. It has been used before. Many years before, in connection with another incident."

"You are going to try to find this Gideon?"

"Yes."

"Even though you are neither a trained nor experienced intelligence officer?"

"Even though," I nodded. "Several experienced professionals have tried, without success. I am what is being called a fresh approach."

"Yes. I understand. Someone who sees things differently, thinks about them differently, without the usual preconceptions.... It could work. Sometimes this approach works, but this is dangerous. It sets the amateur against the professional." He raised his hands immediately. "I mean no disrespect. In other fields you are the professional and I would be the fish that is out of water. Yes? But in this case, you are...."

"Expendable."

"I was going to say vulnerable."

"I can't help that," I countered. "I can only do my best and hope it works out."

"Yes, well, in spite of what I just said, I would not like to have you coming after me. I think you would be imaginative and relentless, that makes you dangerous too."

I smiled my best feral smile.

"Thank you, Emi. I appreciate your help."

"You are welcome, and I will let you 'owe me one' for it. Now, would you like another hot dog?"

I laughed. "You know, I think I would."

When we walked back to the concession stand, Emi ordered two more hot dogs, but when presented with the bill took out a pen and wrote something on it. Then, the pen seemed to jam or run out of ink because he cursed, threw it into a nearby garbage bin and took out a second pen. This pen he laid down on the receipt, then turned to me saying: "Please excuse me, but I seem to have run out of your currency. May I ask you to pay the bill instead?"

"Of course," I replied, taking a couple of bills from my purse and handing them to the server. Then I picked up the pen and receipt and turned towards Emi.

"Keep them. Please. As a small favour to me. A souvenir, if you will."

Odd, I thought, but I thanked him and tucked them into my purse. And with that we gave each other a smile; said 'until the next time,' or something to that effect; then turned and went our separate ways.

It took me a while to walk all the way back around the Forum and down to my seat, but I was able to meld with the crowd and gain my seat just moments before the third period commenced.

"Have a nice walk?" asked Don.

"Very," I replied, but I knew he could hear the concern in my voice. While part of my brain wrestled with how Emi's information fit into the larger jigsaw puzzle, I spared a bit of attention for the third period. The latter wasn't difficult since, if the first and second periods had been rather quiet, this final period was raucous in the extreme as the fans, most of whom were cheering for Team Canada, were doing their best to inspire the players to catch up to the Soviets. Unfortunately, nothing worked, as the Soviets scored five unanswered goals, including a natural hat trick of three goals in a row by Sergei Shepelev. Final score: 8 – 1.

Although the crowd was fairly polite, by hockey standards at least, it was a disappointed crowd that filed out of the Forum that night. Canada had done well overall, of course, having played well throughout the series and finishing in second place, and we found some solace in having the young Wayne Gretzky emerge as the overall scoring leader of the series with 12 points to his credit. The Soviets, for their part, came away as the champions and the best hockey team in the world – for the moment, at least – and I don't think anyone seriously questioned the selection of the Soviets' star goaltender, Vladislav Tretiak, as the Canada Cup's Most Valuable Player (MVP). Tratiak had been outstanding; almost miraculous, and stunning to watch, even if he had been playing for 'the other side.'

After we'd returned to our hotel and said good-night to our shadows: Frank and Sandy, I changed out of my costume and washed most of the makeup off. Then, after first taking Silver outside for a short walk and 'pee break,' Don and I took Ginger out for dinner at a nearby restaurant. All I had told Ginger was that there was someone at the game I'd wanted to meet, and that it had gone well.

It was sometime during dinner, when Ginger had gone off to the ladies' room, that I reached into my purse for a tissue and came up with the receipt Emi had wanted me to keep from the Forum. I looked at it, and thought it was odd that there seemed to be no writing on it. Yet I had seen him writing on it. Then I turn the receipt over. There on the back he'd printed a few words: "For average size and build male, about 2 hours, APPROXIMATELY!!" Frowning, I searched around in my purse and brought out the pen. This time, I looked at it carefully. It was not an ordinary pen.

"Trouble?" asked Don, seeing me frown.

"No. A gift. In fact, a very unexpected gift." I showed him the note. "From Emi" I said. Then, I handed him the pen. "Careful," I warned. "This is no ordinary pen."

Don gave the pen a close inspection, then whistled under his breath. "If this is what I think it is, then this is an extraordinary gift. It appears to be some kind of spy pen, like the on you used to have. Is it lethal?"

"No. It's like the one he gave me after the Diefenbunker case. The one I used in my escape after I'd been captured in Point-du-Chêne last summer[49]. It ejects a dart with a fast-acting tranquilizer. I've seen Emi use them in action. They're very effective."

"He took a big risk giving it to you."

"Yes, he did, and another big risk giving me a new one."

"Exactly the kind of thing 'Jane Bond,' double-oh-one, of Her Majesty's Secret Service would carry with her if there was ever a female Bond movie made."

"Funny you should mention Her Majesty's Secret Service," I said, thoughtfully, looking unfocusedly off in the distance.

"Oh oh. I know that look," said Don. "What crazy thing are you considering now?"

I spotted Ginger returning to our table, so all I said was: "I think its time I met a real MI6 intelligence officer, so we're going to need your Admiral's help."

After Ginger had returned to our table and taken her seat, I said: "I've been scheming again, and I'm going to want you to help me destroy that blonde wig of yours."

Laurie Schramm

5 HER MAJESTY'S SECRET SERVICE

With our Montreal adventure completed, Ginger flew to Vancouver for a screen-test for a new movie, Don flew back to Halifax where he would meet with his admiral, and Silver and I flew back to Ottawa.

It took a few days for Don to meet with Admiral White, and a few more for the admiral to place a few calls to England but, eventually, a path had been cleared and there were two meetings arranged for me in England. I requested a couple of days leave for this, and for something so short no-one bothered to ask me why. This time I would have to leave Silver behind, which I did, in care of a friend in Ottawa.

Getting overseas was somewhat convoluted. I'd been told to pack no more than a medium-sized duffel bag plus a shoulder bag or small backpack. I'd been told I'd be issued new clothes along the way, so I packed only a very few things plus the glasses I'd worn in Montreal, and Ginger's blonde wig, which we had cut short to the point where it would just cover my own hair.

It was a Saturday morning, when I dropped Silver off at my friend's house. With luck, I would be back on the Tuesday evening. I left my truck at my friend's house as well, and was picked up by a black sedan of the type driven by countless senior civil servants in Ottawa. The main differences were that this was a military car, with a military driver, and it was followed at a discreet distance by another such car. Our little convoy took me to the Ottawa Airport, where we went to a medium-sized government terminal building that was off to one side of the much larger public terminal. Inside, I was met by Lieutenant Moore and Sergeant Wilson. I was in civilian clothes, but they were both in uniform. The former in his Air Force blues with wedge cap[50], and the latter in army green and wearing the scarlet beret of the military police.

"Good morning, Ma'am," said Sandy. "We're the security detail for your trip."

"I'm grateful," I said, "but I'm sorry you two seem to be stuck babysitting me again."

"No problem, Ma'am," replied Sandy. They both grinned. "In fact, the chance to fly to England and see the sights isn't exactly rough duty."

"Will I be able to get you two to just refer to me as Alex, at least?"

"Only in private, Ma'am, especially since once we get to Trenton, you're going to outrank us."

"What do you mean?"

"Trust us. We wouldn't want to spoil the surprise." Both grins were switched on again.

"Fine. Are we flying on that monster out there?" There was a huge C-130 Hercules[51] aircraft sitting on the tarmac with its loading doors open.

"Yes Ma'am. It will take us to Trenton[52], where we'll have a short layover, then we'll be travelling by jet to London-Heathrow."

I'd flown on a Hercules before. The noise and vibration were incredible, but it wasn't a long flight, and I'd at least taken the precaution of packing a pair of acoustic earmuffs[53].

When we arrived at the Trenton Air Force Base, it was about 1 pm, so lunch was the next order of business. Following that, we were escorted to a large, warehouse-type building and introduced to a quartermaster sergeant.

"Ah yes," he said, "we have some things for you to try on. Please come with me."

He led me through a part of the building that was packed full with military clothing of all kinds, and for all seasons. Off to one side was an area equipped with chairs, tables, and several doors in proximity. Changing rooms, I presumed.

There was clothing laid-out on one of the tables. "Captain Harrison sent us sizing suggestions, but if you would please try these on, we can change anything that doesn't fit properly." He picked up one of the piles that had been set out on the table.

"A uniform? But I'm not in the service! I was expecting identity papers, not uniforms."

"This is what we were told to issue you with Ma'am. The requisition for the clothes came from Captain Harrison, but they were authorized by Admiral White."

I overheard sniggers from Sandy and Frank, who had followed along to watch the show.

"Look at the epaulettes," said Sandy

I'd been handed what they called No. 3C Service Dress – Sweater, which comprised an open-neck light-blue shirt, a V-neck sweater and dress pants, both in Air Force-blue, black shoes, and all of it topped off with an Air Force-blue wedge cap. On the sweater someone had already attached epaulettes with Captain's bars. This was getting weird!

"We can practice saluting later," said Frank, with a broad grin. Rather than being offended, Sandy and Frank seemed more intent on enjoying my discomfort.

"Admiral's orders, eh?" I grumbled. But I went into a change room and tried everything on, including the shortened blonde wig and the fake glasses. Not surprisingly, since my measurements had been provided by my fiancé, everything fit very well – even the shoes - as the others agreed when I stepped out to look at myself in one of the full-length mirrors that was provided for the purpose.

"Very nice," said the Quartermaster Sergeant approvingly. "I don't think you'll need to try the rest," he said, pointing at the other piles on the table. There were more shirts and socks, a second pair of trousers, a second sweater, a second wedge cap, and an overcoat. The sergeant also gave me a military duffel bag, to use for my new uniforms and also everything I had brought with me in my own suitcase. The duffel bag was made of heavy-duty green canvas, and was cylindrical in shape, with a large zippered main compartment, button-down zipper flap, and transparent ID windows on each end. When I had stuffed everything in, I left my own case with the sergeant, to be picked up when I returned.

"Now for your papers," said the sergeant. "Identification tags, NDI-20, and passport."

The identification tags were what were historically called dog tags; the NDI-20 was a National Defence, Canadian Forces Identification card with my actual photo – except that it was me as a blonde - and listing me as regular officer named MacLerie, Wilhelmina; and the passport wasn't the usual blue one, but a green Special Passport[54]. These had been 'issued' in the name of Wilhelmina MacLerie. There was also a pin-on nametag with white lettering on an air force blue background, that read MacLERIE, but I was advised that this was only provided as a contingency, and not to be affixed to the sweater.

As I put the dog tag chain around my neck, and the nametag in my shirt pocket, I showed the rest of the ID to Sandy and Frank, who had come over for a closer look. "Don's grandmother was Wilhelmina MacLerie. Everyone called her Willie. I guess you'll have to get used to calling me Willie from now on."

"Yes Sir, Captain," they both said. Smiling.

"Is all this really necessary?" I asked.

"Security!" said Sandy, trying to keep a straight face. "Seriously, it was the Admiral's idea. Even if there was a watcher on this base, or at the other end, all they'll see is a bunch of military personnel boarding and deplaning air transport, and customs and passport control in both countries will only know that someone named MacLerie went to England and back."

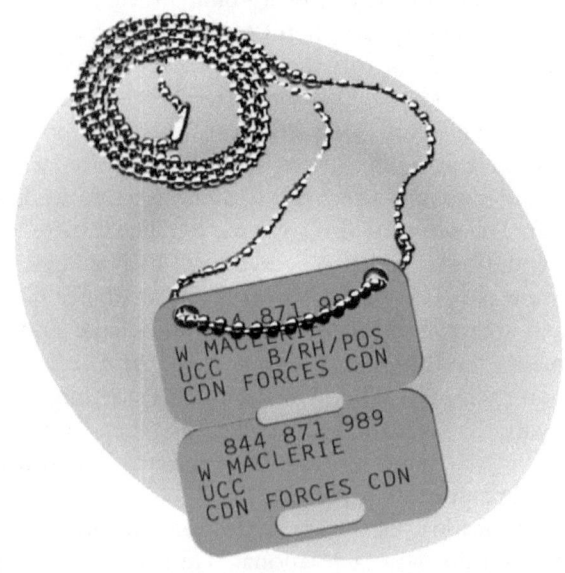

Next, came saluting practice. The Canadian Forces salute is what is sometimes called the 'naval salute' and involves having the palm of the hand turned slightly down and inwards, so the palm is not seen. This is different from the RCMP salute, in which the hand is vertical, with the palm facing directly outwards. We had to practice this several times, before Sandy and Frank were satisfied.

Now feeling more than ever like an actress in dress-rehearsal for a play, I thanked the Quartermaster Sergeant, insisted on carrying my own shoulder bag and duffel, and the three of us went to check-in for our flight. Sandy had all of the paperwork for that, and we checked our duffles, then went for coffee while we waited for departure time, which was about 7 pm.

For the overseas part of our trip, we flew on a Canadian Forces Boeing CC-137, which was a large, four-engine passenger jet[55]. It was quite comfortable and incredibly quiet compared with the noise and vibration aboard a C-130 Hercules.

This time, it was a long, overnight flight and, although I rested, I wasn't able to sleep much. They served us coffee and a light breakfast just before landing though, which helped me focus on the next part of our trip. That and the anticipation of my upcoming meeting.

We landed at a military airport, operated by the RAF, that was located very close to Heathrow Airport. Once we'd cleared security, an RAF Sergeant in plain clothes met and guided us to a BMW full-size sedan, in which he drove us almost due west to the city of Bath.

Of course, I knew that they drove on the left side of the road in the UK, but it was still unnerving to see us being driven on what seemed the wrong side of the road, especially when we had to turn at intersections. The most unsettling of all, however, was when we came to a traffic circle and had to go around in what felt like the wrong lane and in the wrong direction. I was glad I wasn't driving! Had I been driving, I didn't like to think about how many times I'd have had to go around the full circle, before being able to successfully - and safely – navigate the exit.

Most of the trip was on the M4 motorway, which felt very much like being on a divided highway in North America, making it easier to sit back, relax, and enjoy the scenery.

Visiting Bath was like stepping back in history. Named for the famous hot-spring-fed baths built by the Romans *circa*. 60 CE, the older parts of the city have the distinctive narrow streets and many buildings constructed from 'Bath stone,' a creamy-gold coloured limestone.

Major (later promoted to Colonel) Jack Evans (RAF, Ret'd.) lived in Weston, just to the northwest of Bath, a community favoured by retirees. Our driver took us to a very nice-looking two-story, stone apartment building that was surrounded by trees and bushes and bounded on one side by beautiful communal gardens – much like a small park, in fact. He remained in the car while we got out.

Evans was clearly expecting us as he promptly met us at the front door and, following the usual introductions, ushered us through a nicely furnished, large, ground-floor apartment. One wall had floor-to-ceiling windows and windowed-doors looking out on the garden, which was where he ultimately led us.

Immediately outside the door was a small courtyard with some comfortable chairs for us to sit in, while Sandy and Frank went for a stroll in the adjacent communal gardens.

"How about a brew?" he asked. There was a beautiful tea service laid out on a small table between our chairs.

"Yes, please!" I found that I was thirsty after the drive from the airport.

"Standard NATO?" he asked. "Milk and two sugars?"

"No. Just black, if you don't mind." Then: "Would it be possible to get tea for Lieutenant Moore and Sergeant Wilson as well?"

"Take care of the troops and they'll take care of you. Is that it?" It sounded like a test.

"Yes, Sir. We have the same expression."

He seemed to approve and went for two more cups and saucers, waved Sandy and Frank over to a separate table and poured tea for them. Then, as he was pouring the tea for the two of us, I said: "Thank you for agreeing to see me, Colonel."

"My pleasure," he said, handing me my cup. Then, continuing in a lower voice: "Got a call from C himself[56]." He stared at me as if daring me to take the bait.

I didn't. If I didn't already know what 'C' stood for, I think he'd have clammed-up and shown us the door.

When I simply nodded in understanding, he continued. "Special request," he said. "Told me I can tell you anything, within reason of course. There are still a few secrets we don't even tell ourselves," he quipped. "You don't get a call from him unless its damned important, I can tell you, so I agreed. Naturally." He paused, and looked at me rather shrewdly from under a set of very busy eyebrows. "Don't mind telling you it got my curiosity up too. So. What's it all about, eh?"

"Well, Sir," I began. "I want to ask you about something that happened a long time ago, when you were a Military Attaché at the British High Commission."

"Yes. I enjoyed that posting."

"My understanding, is that you received a call in 1959 from someone who offered to sell you the complete plans for the Avro Arrow Jet Fighter."

"Avro Arrow," he mused. "Yes. Your government had just rubbished the whole program and everything was being destroyed to keep it from getting into unfriendly hands. Then, from out of the blue I got a call. A man's voice. Didn't identify himself, naturally, but said he had a set of everything: blueprints, drawings, manuals; the whole lot, in fact. Asked whether we wanted to buy them. I had no idea, of course, but he expected that and said he'd call again in a few days for an answer."

"And you did want to buy them?"

"Yes. After a series of coded cyphers back and forth from higher authority, it was decided that we'd try to buy them. For two reasons, I understood. One was so our people could see the details and possibly incorporate them into a project that was already underway to design a high-altitude, long-range, supersonic fighter that could cross the North Sea to intercept Soviet bombers. That's basically the mission the Arrow was designed for, except across your own northern territories."

"Makes sense. And the second reason."

"Well, to make sure no one else got their hands on them, of course."

"Did you tell our people about all this?"

"Eventually, yes, but not right away. You see our boffins[57] wanted to have a good look at them first. We've always been allies, but there's a limit, what? So, I was instructed to manage the deal, then send everything back home, which is what I did."

"Did any of it actually help you back here?"

"Haven't the foggiest. Probably wouldn't be allowed to tell you even if I did, what? But I believe that everything seemed genuine enough. The source would send us some of the material, for which we'd pay, then call us later to see if we wanted more, and so on. Since everything he gave us was examined and I was always told to go buy the next allotment, I assume it must all have been pretty good stuff."

"And you did eventually tell us about it all."

"Oh yes. Not me. Someone higher up handled all that. I heard that your government didn't even want the plans back. Just asked us to destroy them ourselves so no one else could get at them."

"And did you?"

"I've no idea. I don't think I'd have been told if I'd asked, which I didn't. It was 'need to know' in those days."

"That's one thing that hasn't changed much," I laughed. "Almost no one seems to trust almost anyone."

"Ah, but it was worse in my day, my dear. Much worse."

"What about the source? Did you ever learn anything about who it was?"

"No. Nothing."

"But you must have been curious?"

"Not just curious. I did my damnedest to find out who it was. Would have been quite a feather in my cap if I'd succeeded too. But I didn't."

"Can you tell me about that part of it?"

"I don't see why not. Nothing worth hiding there I don't think…. Let me think for a moment. We used dead-drops for the exchanges. He'd phone me and specify a time and place, and where to look for the latest batch of documents. He wouldn't give me much lead time, so we could arrange stakeouts or anything like that, but we did try having several colleagues travel independently of me, but at the same time, if you take my meaning, to the locations. Then, while I went to pick-up the documents and leave behind an envelope full of money, my colleagues would stick around and take pictures in hopes of photographing whomever went to pick them up later."

"And did you?"

"Who knows?" he said, pounding his fist on one knee for emphasis. "He always picked crowded places, so we ended up with thousands of pictures in which you could make out the faces of some hundreds. We went through them all looking for repetitions at the various drops, but didn't find any."

"So. Everything came to dead-ends then?"

"Everything except the Arrow materials. He delivered everything he said he would, and we paid for all of it. Financially, it was quite a bargain, really. Cost only a tiny fraction of what you chaps would have paid to get all the work done."

"Yes. I've never quite understood why the program was killed-off in the first place. The public story is plausible, but it feels like it may only be a part of the truth."

"Quite likely. Government pronouncements are frequently like that here too." He paused, and looked at me rather shrewdly again.

"On a mole hunt, are we?"

"Sort of. I think of him as a leak. There have been several such leaks spaced out over the years, and my superiors think they – or at least many of them – have come from the same source. It's probably not a mole though. More likely someone out for money, or revenge, or both, rather than anything ideological. As far as we know the Arrow incident was the first of the series."

"Hmmm. Yes, it would have to be something like that to get C to call me and clear the way for you."

"Has no one contacted you before to ask questions like I have, Sir?"

"No," he replied. "You're the first."

"I'm surprised. It seemed so obvious to me."

"Not so surprising if you understand that times were different back then. Look, there have been others before you, who tried to track down your leak, right?"

"Right. Several times, I've been told."

"Well then. In the middle of the Cold War, your predecessors would have been looking for an ideological traitor. Someone with Communist sympathies, that sort of thing. We all were. And they were there too. Right here in Britain, in your country, in the US, in Australia – no one was immune…. Your people must have a list of possible suspects?"

"Yes."

"Well, I won't ask you about it, but it has to be a list of limited size. Your counter-intelligence people of the time may have been looking for the wrong kind of person."

"Yes. No one said so in so many words, but it was kind of implied when I was given the case."

"There you are then. Fresh eyes. New ideas. That kind of thing."

"Yes." I smiled. "That's almost exactly what I was told."

"Thought so." He turned on 'the gaze' again. "And you're not really a Captain in the RCAF are you?"

"What makes you say that?" I asked, involuntarily stiffening a bit.

"I'm not sure." He sat back in his chair and peered at me. "Something about your manner. The way you hold your body. Your way of phrasing things, I think. In fact, now that I think about it, you look and sound more like someone from Scotland Yard than the service. I can't explain myself better than that. It's just a feeling, you see. But I learned to trust my instincts over the years. Seldom let me down if I paid attention to them you know."

Well, I had to hand it to him. After all our precautions, I sit down with him for fifteen minutes and he penetrates my disguise just like that. "Well," I replied. "Since it isn't you that I'm disguised from, I'll admit it."

"Hmmm hmmm. Mounted Police, I'll bet. Security Service maybe?"

"Please never ask me to play poker or chess with you, Sir" I replied. "I'd never be able to afford it."

That brought out a chuckle. "So. You're afraid that your source may be well enough placed to know that you've been set on his trail." It was a statement, not a question.

I nodded yes.

"That explains the security detail." He nodded towards Sandy and Frank, who had returned from their reconnoitre and were standing some distance away, trying to look nonchalant.

"Military intelligence?" he asked.

"That I can neither confirm nor deny," I said, with a smile.

He nodded; his question answered.

"Is there anything else you can remember from the Arrow incident that might help me?"

This time he didn't answer me right away, and I waited while he either searched his memory or mused about how much he could tell me, or both. To be fair, I think it was mostly the former. Eventually, his eyes came back in to focus and he looked directly at me with a gleam in his eyes.

"I asked his name once. Abruptly. Without warning. Figured it was worth a try to see if he'd make a slip. But he didn't. He actually seemed amused ay my clumsy attempt."

"So, it didn't work."

"Yes and no. He said I could call him… let's see now, it was something biblical.…"

I didn't start suggesting names, for fear of derailing his thinking. I just waited.

"Not exactly biblical," he mused, "but close." Then, "I have it," he said, clapping his hands. "Gideon[58]. He said I could call him Gideon." He looked at me closely, watching for a reaction, and he got one. "You've heard the name before, haven't you?"

"I have," I confirmed. "Around the same time, someone using the codename Gideon contacted the USAF offering to sell them the Arrow plans."

"Bollocks! The Yanks had the Arrow secrets all along."

"Yes, so I understand. Apparently, Gideon's offer was simply ignored by the Americans, although the FBI kept the name on file and even had some suspicions about his identity."

The Colonel snorted. "The FBI! They suspected everyone of everything back in Hoover's era."

I nodded.

"Well, there you are. Any more questions?"

I tried to think quickly, but there was only one more question on my mental list. "Just one, I think. All those pictures that were taken at the dead-drops in 1959: is there any chance they still exist?"

"Good question," he replied, approvingly. "We kept everything in those days. The older stuff was boxed-up and stored chronologically. After a certain point it would have been shipped here to headquarters."

"And then?"

"Then? Well, I can't really say for certain.… What I mean is, I don't know. It's possible they were shredded, or burned, at some point, of course. You'd have to ask someone at headquarters, I suppose." He paused, at gave me a significant look. "You do know which headquarters I mean?"

I smiled. "Yes Sir. I think I know exactly which one. I'll go where James Bond would have gone."

"If you can get in, of course."

"I think it can be arranged, Sir," I said with more confidence than I actually felt.

"Yes, I have a feeling you might just pull it off at that." He gave me another penetrating look and then, surprisingly, gave me a conspiratorial grin. "I think you might indeed."

After taking out leave of the Colonel, our driver took us to our hotel in London where we checked in. My first task was to call Don at his office in Halifax. It was just after 5 pm London time, so just after the lunch hour in Halifax.

"How's you day been?" he asked, meaning that plus how my trip overseas had gone.

"A few surprises, but it's been good. I'm calling for some help with my homework."

He caught the code-phrase right away. "I'm tied up right now. Can you call me back in twenty minutes."

I agreed and rung-off. I'd brought my list of phone numbers to use for secret calls to Don, looked up the next unused one, waited twenty minutes and dialed the number. He was right there.

"Hi," came Don's voice on the line.

"Hi yourself. I feel like a fraud in this uniform but the meeting went really well."

"That's great. Did you get anything you can use?"

"Maybe, I don't know. That's why I'm calling. Do you think the Admiral can get me into MI6 to see someone in records or archives, or whatever they call their file storage over here?"

"I have no idea, but I'll ask him. He'll want to know why."

I told him why.

Don whistled. "Talk about a long-shot! But it makes sense since you're over there anyway. I'll try to get in to see him right away. I'll call you as soon as I know something, either late tonight your time, or early tomorrow morning. OK?"

I agreed, and we chatted about more personal things for a while before saying goodbye.

Don's return call to my hotel room came late at night and was circumspect. "It's a go for your homework research tomorrow. No need to dress up, but bring the documents you brought with you."

That meant that I could go visit MI6, that I wasn't to go in uniform, but that I was to use the MacLerie persona and its passport and military ID.

The next morning, after breakfast, the same car and driver picked us up and took us to the headquarters of Britain's Secret Intelligence Service, popularly known as MI6[59]. It was less than a block away from the Lambeth North Tube Station, but Sandy and Frank had vetoed my idea of taking The Tube[60] on security grounds.

Taking our cue from Don, we were all in business-casual clothes, although I still thought that Frank looked like a sergeant in somebody's army in any kind of clothes. I supposed that in this case, it didn't really matter. I retained the blonde wig and glasses of my disguise from the previous two days.

Our identities were carefully checked against a list twice, once at the main gate, and again just inside the main entranceway. From there we were given visitor passes to wear and someone escorted us to a bank of elevators and up to the 21st floor, which was the second highest. This floor had unusually high ceilings and seemed to comprise a reception area and a number of large meeting rooms.

In the centre of the floor, to one side of the elevators, was a staircase, and beside that, an ornate desk that could have been from the Victorian era. At it sat an alert-looking, middle-aged woman. *Shades of Moneypenny*[61], I thought to myself, and had to concentrate to avoid grinning. The whole thing seemed so surreal to me.

The woman at the desk didn't identify herself, but once again carefully checked our identities against a list, which I suspected contained physical descriptions in addition to ID and passport identification numbers. While she did that, I glanced around wondering about enhanced security, and I noticed that there were a couple of offices facing us that had a clear view of the elevators, the staircase, and the desk at which we were standing. The fronts of the offices had floor-to-ceiling glass windows and glass doors, with the glass doors standing open. Sitting inside each office was a heavily-built man that looked reminiscent of Sergeant Wilson. Both men seemed to find us fascinating, as they never seemed to take their eyes off of us.

My thoughts in this direction were interrupted by the woman at the desk who, having completed her identity checks, picked up her phone, dialed a number and whispered something we couldn't hear. Then she said: "Captain MacLerie, the Chief would like a word with you."

"Of course," I replied.

"I'm sorry, but the Lieutenant and the Sergeant will have to wait here for you."

I glanced at the two men, who both nodded and strode over to some comfortable-looking chairs to settle-in and wait.

The woman from the desk nodded to the person that had escorted us up from the main entrance, who left, and then led me up the staircase to the top floor. At the top of the stairs, and set back only a few metres, was a solid wall with large, glass double doors. Sitting at desks on either sides were two more heavily-built men, with the same intent look and lack of facial expression that the two in the offices a floor below wore. Presumably, the body language of the woman guiding told them that nothing was amiss, because neither of the men seem to move a muscle as we went through the doors.

On this floor, there were windows right in front of us, and a solid wall, each with a solid door, on each side of us. It was to one of these doors that I was led and, after a discreet knock on the door, I was ushered in.

It was silly of me, I know, but having read my share of spy novels I actually expected to see a dimly lit alcove with an old, greying man hunched over a small desk, surrounded by piles of files and papers. Possibly even smoking an old pipe. This was completely wrong, of course.

The first thing that caught my attention was the man himself. He wasn't old. *Middle-aged*, I judged. Even sitting, he appeared tall and somewhat on the slender side. He had blond hair and ice-blue eyes.

His office was far from my imagined image too. The office I really entered was large and bright, with two of the walls being completely glass, offering stunning views of the city. There was a very modern desk just off-centre, and in one corner there was a small meeting table with four comfortable-looking chairs around it. A quick glance around his office showed the remaining walls were covered by bookcases, with souvenirs or ornaments on some of the shelves, but mostly just books. Lots of books, in fact. I would have liked to look at them to see their titles, or if they were even real. The bookcases, like the rest of the office furniture were made of gleaming chrome and glass. Everything, in fact, seemed bright and clean. New, even.

Although I tried to take everything in, my attention was focused on the man himself. Rather than waiting for our approach, he sprung up from his desk and came round to greet me, saying: "Welcome, please come and take a seat." He motioned to the small meeting table. "Can we offer you something to drink?"

"Yes, thank you. Tea would be nice."

He was dressed in a fashionable business suit that would not have looked out of place if he was walking around the business and financial district of the city.

He gazed at me with a smile. "You don't have to drink tea just to be accommodating, you know. We do have such things as coffee around here... somewhere."

I smiled in return. "Actually, I am a dedicated coffee drinker, but I've been enjoying the change so I really would prefer tea if that's OK."

"Of course." He nodded to his assistant who left to get my tea. She obviously didn't have to ask him for his own preference.

"Now then. Captain MacLerie. Or, should I say Corporal Houston?"

"Either Sir. I can't say I'm surprised that you know who I really am."

"No. Peter White had a lot to say about you." He motioned to a small cabinet beside his desk, that had just one thing on it: an ordinary looking telephone set.

Appearances can be deceiving. That cabinet, I knew would be filled with racks of electronics. "A scrambler phone."

"Indeed. What the Americans call a STU phone."

"Yes, Sir. My Deputy Commissioner has one in his office, I'm sure the Admiral has one too."

"Just so. Very handy for frank conversations, I find."

We were interrupted by his assistant, who softly knocked and brought us our tea, then discreetly left.

"I'll refer to you as Captain, to keep things simple. No one else in this building knows anything else about you or why you're here, except that you're Canadian. If they harbour any suspicions about why you have a Lieutenant and a Sergeant following you around like guard dogs, well, it wouldn't be the first time someone has come for a meeting here accompanied by a security detail. Right?"

"Yes, Sir."

"Now then, how was your meeting with Colonel Evans?"

75

"It went well, I think, although he mostly just confirmed what I already suspected. The same codename – Gideon - seems to keep popping up for our leak, which could be helpful. Our meeting did reassure me that I may be going in the right direction, which is always a help, too."

"And now I understand that you want to delve into our archives."

"Yes, Sir. Your Consulate people in Ottawa took a huge number of pictures at the dead-drops. I know that nothing came from that exercise but...."

"You think you might actually recognize one of the faces in the pictures, don't you? Something our chaps would never have been able to do."

"That's my hope, Sir. Yes. Now that I know what all of our 'possibles' look like, I'm hoping I'll get lucky and spot one of them in the pictures. If they still exist, and if we can find them in your archives, that is."

"Do you know how many pictures were taken at the time?"

"Thousands, the Colonel estimated."

His eyebrows went up. "A tall order then, I'm afraid." He looked at me, as if weighing things in his mind, then he seemed to reach a decision. "Right then. I agree it's worth a try. We don't let people into our files and archives lightly, of course[62], but I think we'll let you have a go."

He got up, and walked over to his desk and reached inside the knee-hole, presumably to press a button. Before long, his assistant knocked and entered.

"Take Captain MacLerie down to meet our librarian, would you? Tell him to call me if he has any questions."

"Yes, Sir," she replied and went to the door to wait for me.

"Nice to have met you, Captain. I'd most likely have honoured Peter White's request in any case, but I wanted to meet you in person first. Take your measure, as we say." He offered his hand, which surprised me.

"Thank you very much, Sir," I acknowledged, shaking his hand with a firm grip.

He noticed that too.

"Good luck," he said, but he'd already turned back to his desk, his mind having shifted to other things.

As we walked down the stairs, C's assistant told me that it wasn't really a library to which we were heading, but that they tended to refer to their massive collection of files and documents as the library, rather than its official designation. The Head of Section, was similarly referred to as "L," their librarian.

At the bottom of the stairs, I went to check-in with Sandy and Frank, telling them that I had one more stop, and that it might take me several hours. They replied that they were "doing just fine, Ma'am."

C's assistant then guided me to the main elevators, one of which took us down several floors. As we exited the elevator, we entered a floor that reminded me of a large university library. Most of the floor seemed to be taken up by floor-to-ceiling shelving on which were arranged books, document cases, and even file boxes. Closer to where we were standing, to one side, was a bank of desk-stations that seemed to be hybrid computer terminals and scanning stations. At each sat an operator scanning files and documents page-by-page. *Digitizing paper records*, I thought. To the other side was a bank of more conventional-looking computer terminals at which operators seemed to be busily alternating between typing things and then peering intently at the computer monitors. *Digital search and document retrieval*, I thought.

Directly in front of us were a couple of desks that looked exactly like librarian's desks in a conventional library. Just past the computer stations, was a glass-enclosed office, and it was to this that I was led.

"Good morning, L," said C's assistant to the man who was seated at a desk in the office. He was elderly, I thought, probably well past the normal retirement age, and he was definitely not dressed as fashionably as the other I had met that morning. In fact, he reminded me very much of the retired chemistry professors that had volunteered their time to help my student colleagues and I grapple with the concepts and laws of thermodynamics, in my university days. Old, soft-looking shirts, corduroy trousers, topped off with a sleeveless, V-neck sweater had been our mentors' dress code, and this man seemed to have come from the same mold. He even had a shock of unruly white hair, with bushy white eyebrows to match.

I tried hard not to stare.

"This is Captain MacLerie" said C's assistant. "C asks that you try to help her out, and to call if you have any concerns."

"How do you do, my dear," said the man, as he got up from his seat and came around the desk to shake hands.

"How do you do, Sir," I replied.

"Now, now. No need for formality down here. People call me L. It's not my real title, but that's not important."

"L for librarian?" I asked, as C's assistant silently glided away.

"Of course," he said, as if surprised that anyone would ask. "You probably noticed the scanning stations and computer terminals as you walked in?" He peered over the tops of his glasses inquisitively.

I nodded.

"Right. Everything's going digital these days, and of course we're scanning the most current records first and then working backwards, so it will be many years before we get to the old stuff. That's why I'm still here, and why they call me L." He tapped his head significantly. "Until the computers make me obsolete, I'm the retrieval system, especially for the really old stuff. It's all filed away in me. Been here through every C we've ever had, I have. Right back to the original one."

"How do you manage to keep it all straight," I asked, "besides being able to remember it all?"

"Well, I can't really remember everything, can I?" he asked, with a twinkle in his eyes. "But I have a good memory for most things, and a pretty good feeling for dates and events, so I'm usually pretty close, and then it's the old method of sifting through papers by hand after that. I'm a bit of a ferret once I get started, and I usually find what people are looking for in the end. Not always on time, you understand, but I do generally get there.... Let's put me to the test, shall we? What might it be that you're after?"

"I'm hoping you will have retained a large collection of photographs," I said, and I launched into a description.

"Canada, you say... 1959... Avro Arrow and the Consulate. Hmmm. Major Jack Evans. Yes, I remember him all right, the young puppy. Hmmm. Well, they may have been shredded or burned long ago, you understand?"

"Yes, I know. But I'm hoping they weren't."

"Well, if they still exist then we have them, but not here. Come with me." With that he led me back to the elevators and we went down, way down, to one of several basement levels.

When we arrived and exited the elevator, it was like we'd left one world and entered another. This world was only dimly lit and consisted almost entirely of row upon row of floor-to-ceiling racks containing storage boxes. Although the building was quite modern, this level smelled old.

Noticing me take it all in, L said: "Yes, you can feel the age of things down here, can't you? It puts some people off, especially the ones with allergies, but not me. This is where I feel most at home. Have a seat," he pointed to a couple of old desks and equally old-looking hardwood chairs, "and let me nose around a bit. I'll call you when I find something."

So, I took a seat and waited. I didn't expect him to find anything right away, but it was at least 45 minutes before he came back carrying an old file box.

"You found them?" I asked.

"Could be. Could be. We'll see in a moment." He placed the box on the desk, switched on the desk lamp and opened it up. At the front was a file folder, which he extracted and quickly perused. "Report of Surveillance, Source: Gideon, Location: Ottawa, June, 1959," he said, and then handed the file to me. As I read the brief report, L looked through the rest of the box. "Photographs!" he said, "hundreds and hundreds of them."

"Fantastic!" I said. "I'm looking for a face."

"Description?"

"I have no idea," I responded. Then, "I'm looking for a face that I recognize."

"Ah. I see. You'll be here for a while then." He opened a drawer and took out a large magnifying glass. "This might help. While you start on these, I'll go back for the other boxes."

"Other boxes?"

"There are two more. I would say you're going to be looking at more than 3,000 photographs."

It didn't go quite as slowly as I first thought. Some of the photos didn't show any clear facial details, some didn't show people at all, and some were so poorly focused that I wondered why they had been kept at all. It took me an hour to go through everything in the first box and, since the photos were numbered, I knew that I had looked at over 900 of them.

L had brought back two more boxes for me to go through, and I was about to start on the second when someone arrived with a thermos of tea and some paper cups.

"Take frequent breaks," L advised. "I know what it feels like when the hunt is on, but if you push too far you can't help but lose focus and before you know it, you're glossing over the very things that should be getting your most careful attention."

This sounded like good advice to me, so I thanked him and poured myself a cup. "Would you care to join me?" I asked.

"Don't mind if I do, actually. I'm not allowed to leave you alone down here anyway. Never know what you colonials might get up to, what?"

I didn't take offense. His smile could have been misinterpreted, but his tone told me he was joking.

So, I did take breaks, during which he told me some hair-raising stories of old cases that had been completed due, in no small part, to his ability to 'ferret-out' valuable intelligence from their massive 'library' collection.

I took periodic breaks after that, but by the time I'd gone through the second box, I was getting tired and hungry. L offered to take me upstairs for lunch, but I was in a groove, of sorts, and wanted to see the whole collection first. L just nodded. He understood, and he settled back companionably enough, to wait.

I was probably about halfway through the third box, when I gasped and my whole body stiffened.

"Found something, have you?" queried L.

"Maybe. It's out of focus, and only part of the face is visible, but it reminds me of someone."

"Often the case," muttered L. "Your Gideon has been through multiple dead-drops, multiple exchanges, the money's adding up, and he's beginning to relax. The one thing an agent must never do. But they all do, sooner or later, otherwise we'd never catch them. Not the smart ones, anyway. Keep going, but carefully now. If he's slipped up once, he'll do it again."

Nothing could have stopped me at that point. I'd come too far. As I finished scanning each photo, I'd eagerly reach for the rest, but it was probably a hundred photos later that my body froze again as I came across what appeared to be the same face, partly obscured and from a different angle, but it looked like the same face.

"Another hit?' L asked, but I simply nodded as I continued on.

It took another two hundred photos, before I found it – he must have chanced to look in exactly the direction of the camera. He was wearing a hat, but otherwise his whole face could be clearly seen, and it was in sharp focus.

"Here it is," I said, passing the photo to L and pointing out the face I'd recognized out of the thousands of others.

"You don't look very happy," L observed.

"I'm not at all happy," I agreed.

"You know who this is?"

"Yes. I know who it is."

Laurie Schramm

6 A NEW ASSIGNNMENT

I'd had lots of time to think on the way home, and had devised and discarded quite a few convoluted schemes for getting Gideon into the open and compromised. As we landed, I still hadn't come up with anything that seemed realistic and I tried to put it out of mind for a while, hoping that my subconscious mind would eventually produce inspiration.

I did, however, drop by Staff Sergeant Blunt's office for a quiet chat one day and I told him that I was still working on the case.

"But it wasn't me that...."

"I know," I interrupted.

"I can't prove it, but I assure you that... wait a minute. What do you mean you know?"

"I mean, I know who it is, and it's not you, OK?"

He looked at me. "What do you want then?"

"I'm asking for your help. To play along with this, when the time comes, so we can catch the real Gideon."

"Who is it?"

"Trust me? Please? If you know who it is, you'll react differently to things, and our quarry will bolt. OK?"

"He made a sour face. "I suppose I don't have much choice, do I?"

"Look, I'm not threatening you. You can just walk away. Right? I'll still try to prove it wasn't you and catch the real Gideon."

He looked at me again, but this time as if I'd just passed some kind of test. "No, no. Not on your life. Count me in... Alex."

Now, again, I needed to wait for an opportunity, so I worked on a number of routine cases that came up. Not all of them were exactly routine, however.

Several weeks later, for example, I was in my office typing reports when Bob called me into his office.

"Uncle George got a call from the FBI," he began. "Last week, there was a break-in at a National Guard armory near Houston, Texas. Whomever it was got away with a load of weapons crates. The crates contain M203 under-barrel grenade launchers[63] designed to be mounted on the U.S. M16 rifle, or the Canadian C7. The FBI traced them as far as the Port of Houston, but by the time they arrived in force, it was too late: the goods had vanished. They think the weapons were loaded onto an unregistered ship that was anchored out in the harbour, then taken out through the Gulf of Mexico.

"They have a general description, but not a positive ID on the ship, which was last seen disappearing into a storm that covered most of the Gulf of Mexico in dense cloud. A couple of days ago, they found three unidentified cargo ships passing the southern tip of Florida and heading for international waters. The three ships seem to have been heading more-or-less north along the west coast, all of them outside of the 12-nautical-mile territorial limit, and the US Coast Guard has been watching out for them."

"OK," I said. "What do they want from us?"

"Today, one of the ships has been spotted off the New England coast, but still in international waters, and they think it may be intending to cross into Canadian waters."

"Sounds like a job for our Coast Guard and maybe a few people from H or B Division[64]."

"Normally yes, but here's where it gets interesting. Apparently, the CIA think that one of the crates is a dummy and really contains some kind of new, experimental explosive shells that were stolen from a research lab at the armory at the same time."

"How big is this thing?"

"The crate contains two specially modified M549[65] rocket-assisted howitzer rounds," said Bob, reading from a sheet of paper in his hand. "Each round is 155 mm (6.1") diameter, nearly a metre (33") in length, and weighs about 40 kg (88 lbs). That means the crate weighs more than twice that.

"No one will admit anything, but the FBI think that the bomb-

84

in-a-crate thing was actually a CIA operation. The suspicion is that they were intending to ship it somewhere for experimental use, but someone got wind of it and stole the whole shipment."

"If that were true, why not steal just the one important crate? It would have been a lot easier to disguise and transport."

"I asked the FBI that. They suspect that the thieves were hired to steal the weapons by an arms dealer, or someone posing as one, and that they don't know anything about the special crate."

"Sounds like a plot from a James Bond novel."

"I agree, but Deputy Director Wheeler called Uncle George directly over this. He has his reservations too, but the CIA is apparently major-league cranky over this, despite denying any involvement of course. The U.S. Army is doubly upset, partly because the shipment was stolen from their facility and partly because they also think they were being used as dupes by the CIA. The U.S. Coast Guard is under pressure to find the right ship, and the FBI is under pressure to reel it in. If that isn't enough, the FBI doesn't want to get caught in the crossfire of a nasty inter-service battle between the CIA and the U.S. Army."

"OK," I said, "That part makes sense at least."

"Right. So. If the ship crosses into our waters, then it's like you said. Our Coast Guard will take over, backed-up by the navy if necessary, and H Division will put someone on the Coast Guard ship."

"And…" I prompted, waiting for the punch-line.

"None of them are allowed to know anything about the possibility of a secret cargo in one of the crates, nor anything about its contents, and especially nothing about any possible CIA involvement. In fact, the CIA asked – ordered is more like it – the FBI to keep us in the dark too, but Director Wheeler told Uncle George anyway. Said he'd never send one of his own Special Agents in half-blind and he wasn't about to start doing it to us either."

"Ah ha. And you want me to go."

Bob smiled his Cheshire Cat smile. "Everybody wants you and Silver to go: Uncle George, Director Wheeler, me, and the Special Agent they're sending in." He paused for a moment, to make sure I had it all straight in my mind.

"Let me guess."

"Right. Special Agent Vivian Rule."

"All right. I suppose Silver makes some sense since we're looking for explosives again. You realize, of course, that if it's a really new kind of explosive then Silver might not be able to detect it or recognize it for what it is. Can we get a sample, or some information on the chemical components?"

"No. For two reasons. One, that we're not supposed to know anything about it. The FBI wasn't supposed to tell us. Secondly, the CIA won't tell the FBI anything about it either, nor the U.S. Army, nor their own Coast Guard."

"Makes you wonder who's side they're on, doesn't it?"

"I'll pretend I didn't hear you say that," said Bob, with a straight face. The he switched his smile back on again. "Any other questions?"

"Tons. I suppose we also don't know how the thing is supposed to be triggered or detonated, or handled for that matter, or its explosive power?"

"Nope, but it's a safe bet the thing is powerful. Everyone is way too upset for it to be anything less."

"Great."

"OK. Uncle George says to ask...."

"I know, 'Will I do it?'"

Bob smiled.

"Why me?" I asked, rhetorically, as I raised my hands in surrender.

"Fine," said Bob. He'd expected my answer. He waited until I'd stood up before adding: "One more thing Alex," he said. "With the CIA this upset, and everyone running around in circles, we have to assume it's all pretty important. That means other parties may take an interest as well. Our usual opponents, anarchist groups, real arms dealers, extremists. Any or all of them might be just as anxious to get their hands on the thing, whether for its own sake or the money that could be made by selling it."

"If they know about it."

Bob sighed. "We have to assume they do. You know that. Look how many people know about it already that aren't supposed to. It's only a matter of time before rumours begin to expand and travel."

"Riiight."

I started for the door, then paused and turned back towards Bob's desk as I realized I'd missed something. "If the CIA's in such a snit and pushing everyone around so much, don't you think they'd send in one of their own agents as well?"

"I wouldn't be the least bit surprised," said Bob, approvingly.

"Great."

"You're going to be out in the open on this one, so keep me informed as best you can, and call out if you need anything. Right?"

"Right."

Our next steps saw Silver and I fly to Halifax where we boarded a navy destroyer, the *HMCS Assiniboine*[67]. I was told that a local constable from H Division was already aboard.

It turned out to be Constable Jack McDonald. This was good news, but I wasn't completely surprised as it wasn't the first time Uncle George and/or Bob had arranged for Jack to be close at hand when I was going into something that could be unusually dangerous.

A Chief Petty Officer showed me to my quarters so I could stow my gear. It turned out that one of the ship's officers had been moved to make a cabin available for Silver and I. When that was done he escorted me to the bridge so I could make a courtesy call on the ship's captain. Silver and I had been on Canadian destroyers before, so Silver and I were then set free to roam about the ship, and I'd found Jack playing cards, cribbage in this case, with some sailors in the Chiefs' and Petty Officers' Mess.

"What's going on, Alex?" asked Jack. "I've been briefed, but something tells me there was more going on than meets the eye, and now 'the penny drops[67]' with you showing up!"

"Like a bad penny?" I asked, with a grin. Then, more seriously:

"when you've finished your game, let's take a walk."

"I've already lost this one," he said ruefully, standing up and tossing a five-dollar bill onto the board. "Besides, I don't get paid enough to be able to play crib with these sharks."

The two petty officers he'd been playing with tried to put innocent expressions on, but there were telltale gleams in their eyes.

"What's that all about? You almost never lose at crib," I said as we walked down several passageways, heading for the stern of the ship.

He smirked. "I thought that if I lost a game or two, it might make me less of an intruder and more of a colleague onboard."

"Ah ha. So speaks the real shark. Even I know better than to play crib with you for money."

Jack chuckled. Then, more soberly asked: "So, what's up?"

I waited until we were out in the open, on the helicopter landing pad, which was also our primary location for Silver to pee because it was so easy to clean-up after him there. Then, I turned to him and picked up the tale.

"Well, you're right," I began. "There is more going on than meets the eye, and everything is on a 'need to know' basis."

"That's the case for almost everything in your line of work!"

"Almost," I agreed, "and I'm not supposed to admit anything to anybody except in case of emergency. But!" I held up a hand to forestall the protests that were making their way to Jack's lips. "I want you to know. So, what I'm NOT telling you is…." I told him some of what I knew to be going on, and quite a bit of what I suspected. But I didn't tell him everything. Maybe if I had, he'd still be alive today. I'll never know, and it will haunt me for the rest of my life.

After our confidential chat, and with the help of a passing sailor, we were able to find the executive officer, who took us to see the ship's captain.

The captain had been briefed on the three mystery ships, the possibility that one of them was carrying stolen armaments from the American armory, and that the U.S. Coast Guard had been trying to locate them.

"Isn't there some kind of tracking device for large ships?" I asked.

"No[68]. Even if there was, this kind of ship would simply switch it off."

"I suppose. Can the ships be followed by a spy satellite then?"

"Not easily. The Americans have a number of Big Bird[69] satellites up, but even if one passes our target and photographs it, we won't know about it until the film is dropped on one of the satellite's four recoverable re-entry vehicles, then caught by an aircraft in mid-air while it parachutes down, then analyzed back on earth. Instead, the U.S. Navy has been using Vigilante reconnaissance aircraft[70].

A U.S. Navy RA-5C Vigilante Reconnaissance Aircraft

"Until recently, the cloud cover was too dense for the aircraft to spot the ships except sporadically. Now that the weather has begun to clear, they have found one of the ships in international waters due east of New York and heading north-north-east."

"Heading towards us, you mean," I said.

"As of the latest aerial photos, yes. The Americans have sent the *USCGC Decisive*[71] to find it and keep it under observation. Initially they'll use their radar but the ship carries a helicopter, like we do, so they'll use that to make a visual confirmation that it matches the description provided by the FBI in Texas. Once they've located and identified the ship, they have been ordered to keep well back, out of sight, and follow it on radar."

"Will the freighter be able to use their radar to figure out that they're being followed?"

"Not if the *Decisive* is careful. Their radar is more powerful than the freighter's."

"What are your orders, Captain?"

"We are to cast-off at dawn tomorrow and head south on an interception course, except that we won't be intercepting them. Instead, we are to remain out of sight and off their radar and help keep an eye on them. We can do that because our radar will have at least twice the range of the freighter.

"If the ship stays in international waters and heads for Europe or Africa, say, then we return to port. Same thing happens if they turn around and head for the southern states or South America. If, on the other hand, it looks like they are going to head for our waters and make for one of our ports, then an FBI liaison agent will be transferred to us and we'll follow them in."

As announced, we cast-off at dawn the next morning with Jack, Silver, and I up to sightsee as we made our way out of the harbour. At this point, we were nearly 600 nautical miles from the mystery freighter, with us cruising roughly southeast at about 12 knots and the freighter heading toward us at about 11 knots. Depending on reports from the U.S. Coast Guard, the captain therefore expected that it would be sometime on the second day before we learned much new about the probable destination of the freighter.

By the next morning, the freighter was still on a direct heading for Nova Scotia, or perhaps Newfoundland, and we were getting close, so the destroyer swung out towards the open sea in order to avoid being spotted. By mid-day, we were summoned to the bridge where the captain explained he had been advised that the freighter was southeast of Lunenberg, Nova Scotia, and that it was still in international waters but beginning to turn towards Halifax.

"Assuming that they are heading for Halifax," he said, "my orders are to rendezvous with the *Decisive*, and bring the FBI Agent onboard. Once they cross into our waters, law enforcement will be up to you and the FBI Agent will serve as liaison. The *Decisive* has a helicopter, and will use that to transfer the agent."

"OK. Thank you," I said. "I know the agent. It will be Special Agent Vivian Rule. May I ask what are your orders are regarding the freighter?"

"You may ask. Perhaps you can even explain them to me," he said, with a growl. "I'm to continue to stand off, remain out of their radar range, and observe while rendering you all possible assistance short of endangering the ship. Seems crazy to me, but I'm just the captain. No one has explained anything to me," he complained. His tone and expression made it clear that he wasn't joking.

I didn't want him to be too grumpy because I needed that assistance he was supposed to provide, so I said: "May we have a word in private, Captain?"

He nodded brusquely and led Jack and I to the back of the bridge.

"OK," I began. "You know that the freighter is suspected of carrying crates of military weapons that were stolen from an armory in Texas."

He nodded.

"So it is, but what I'm not allowed to tell you is that at least one of those crates may contain some kind of new, top-secret explosive mounted in howitzer shells. It has something to do with the CIA, and apparently, they're upset and crawling all over the FBI. Whatever this new thing is, the CIA don't want the freighter to toss it overboard when they see a coast guard or navy ship approaching. Instead, they want the ship to be able to dock and offload it. Then it will be our job to find out who it's being shipped to and then recover it before anyone else can."

"Sounds like a tall order to me, but someone must think it's important to take the risk of the thing blowing up in the harbour!"

I nodded, soberly.

"OK then," he sighed. "What do you need from me?"

"Once it's clear that it's heading for the harbour, would you have your helicopter take us up, get ahead of the freighter, drop Jack off on Georges Island[72], and then drop Vivian, Silver, and I at the berth we cast-off from at the dockyard?"

"That's all?"

"Well, I'd also like to make a couple of radiotelephone calls, but otherwise that's all."

The captain agreed, I made my calls, and then we all had to wait.

Within an hour, as Jack, Silver, and I stood by the helideck near the stern of the destroyer, we could hear the sound of a large Sikorsky helicopter approaching. It was from the *Decisive*, and touched down just long enough for Vivian to disembark and grab her duffel bag. Then, with an increasing roar, it lifted off again, angled back and away from the destroyer, then turned and headed back to its own ship.

When the noise from the helicopter had abated a bit, Silver and I were able to greet Vivian properly. We had worked together on three previous cases, but she and Jack hadn't crossed paths yet, so I introduced them. With that done, we went off to find a quiet place to catch up on any new details regarding the case.

It seemed like no time before we were called to the bridge and advised that the *Decisive* had radioed to say that the freighter was entering the outer reaches of the harbour. The captain seemed relieved to be nearing the end of this particular assignment, for him at least, and even managed a smile when we offered our thanks and goodbyes.

As we left, I heard him say: "Helmsman, stay alert when we enter the harbour. We don't want to run aground again[73]."

Maybe he has a sense of humour after all, I thought.

As soon as we had piled into the *Assiniboine's* helicopter, along with our gear, the pilots started it up and we were soon in the air. When we arrived at the mouth of the harbour, the pilots remained over water, but kept to the northeast shore (the Dartmouth side) and tried to look like just one more military helicopter flying toward the dockyard and other military facilities known collectively as CFB Halifax.

"There she is. Directly to port," came the voice of the co-pilot over the headphones that we'd all been given. As we peered out and down, we could see an older-style freighter in the sea-lane. Any cargo that it was carrying was stowed below decks because there was nothing to see up top, just streaked, fading paint and lots of rust.

We passed the freighter, landed Jack on the northern tip of Georges Island, out of sight of the freighter, and then continued to the naval dockyard where Vivian, Silver and I, and our gear were deposited. With a wave, the pilots took off and headed back to their ship, while the rest of us went and stored our gear in the unmarked police SUV that I had parked there previously. Then, we walked back to the *Assiniboine's* empty pier and I tried calling Jack on the hand-held VHF radios we each had. We were each equipped with powerful binoculars, as well.

"Great visibility from the old fort," said Jack. "The freighter is just passing McNabs Island now." This, I knew, was the larger island, which was positioned near the mouth of the harbor.

"She's still headed my way, and is about two kilometres from my position."

About 15 minutes later came another update. "She's just at my position now. Can't be doing much more than about 6 knots. Obviously not heading for the Ocean Container docks."

After another 15 minutes: "Must be just about at your position now. Looks like she may be heading for the Bedford Basin. The police boat is here for me now. We'll follow her, but keep about 2 kilometres back."

At this point we all got into my SUV and drove to the North Marginal Road, which passes underneath the A. Murray Mackay Bridge, the most northerly of the two bridges that connect Halifax to its sister city of Dartmouth. There was a bit of a park there, that afforded us a great view of the bridge, the most northerly part of The Narrows, and the expanse of the Bedford Basin.

The freighter must have slowed down even more, because it was half an hour before we received another radio report from Jack.

"It's approaching the Mackay Bridge. If you're where I think you are, you should see it any minute."

"Got it," I acknowledged. "It's coming under the bridge now. Maybe it's going to anchor out in the basin. That will sure complicate things for us."

As I watched the freighter through my binoculars, thoughts of trying to deal with the ship at anchor were flying through my head. I was just wondering whether we'd be able to get approval for an armed boarding party when I realized that the ship was turning towards me.

"Careful Jack. The ship is turning. If they're not heading for the Fairview Docks behind me, then they might be turning completely around so they can get to the Richmond Docks[74]."

As I watched in fascination, the ship came about an entire 180 degrees and headed back towards the bridge.

"They're definitely heading back towards the bridge, Jack. It's got to be making for the Richmond Docks. If you can keep an eye on them from the water, we'll drive as close as we can. We'll need to know the exact dock they tie-up at."

"Right," he said.

Before long, we were able to radio H Division headquarters, downtown, with the exact position of the freighter and also to make arrangements to have it closely watched as it began unloading its cargo. With those arrangements made, we drove back to the naval dockyard to pick up Jack and head for an office from which we could plan our next steps.

When we got there, the first thing I did was phone my boss, Bob to update him. He wasn't in the office, but I was able to leave a detailed message for him before I went back to our meeting.

While we were discussing tactics, the first watchers were sent out. The ideal observation position for the cargo unloading was up on the Mackay Bridge, but there were no pedestrian or bike lanes on that bridge. For that reason, a large highways truck made its way up onto the eastbound lane and wasn't far along the bridge before it pulled over to the curb and parked, with its two flashing amber lights operating and an illuminated highways sign carrying an arrow that indicated to other traffic that they should move over and pass on its left-hand side.

As most of the following traffic moved over to comply, a plain van passed and then turned in to park just ahead of the highways truck. This was an unmarked police van, with no emergency lights switched on at all. The two plainclothes officers inside simply opened the rear doors and set up - within the van but looking towards the Richmond Docks – two reasonably comfortable folding chairs, one of each mounted behind a tripod-mounted spotting scope and a tripod-mounted camera. That done, they settled in to take turns watching the freighter until the next shift would come to relieve them. This went on for some time, because the freighter began unloading cargo and continued to do so well into the evening.

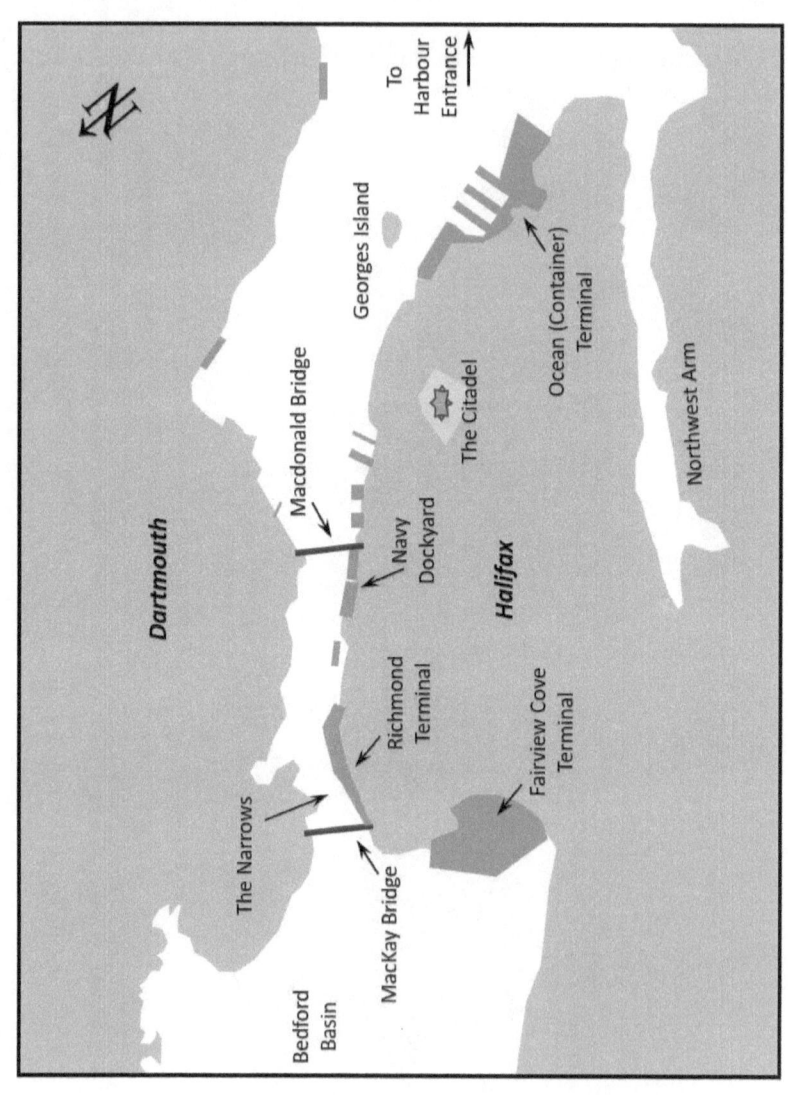

7 CONVERGENCE

Betrayal may come from within.

Moscow Rules (see Endnote 1).

A phone began to ring in a Halifax hotel room. It was just past midnight, but the occupant was awake. He'd been waiting for this call.

"Hello?"

"Hi Avery. Bob here. I just got word on the crates from the freighter." There was noise on the line, but the words could be understood.

"You know where they are?'

"I think so. We had to wake up a lot of people at the terminal authority, and they did a lot of complaining, but we finally got what we need. Unless somebody screwed-up, the crates should be in the northeast corner of Warehouse A. That's the north one. Got it?"

"I think so," said Staff Sergeant Blunt, writing on a pad beside the phone. "Northeast corner, north building, which is Warehouse A. You think someone will try for it tonight?"

"Hard to say from all the way back here in Ottawa," Bob paused for a moment, as if in thought. "But the FBI seem to think the receiver

is going to be in a hurry. That might mean it's the CIA that thinks that, or maybe it means it's the CIA that's nervous. Who the hell know? You're the counter-intelligence expert, not me."

"Thanks a lot. You're saying you don't think we should take any chances." It was a statement, not a question.

"Well, no, I don't. Do you?"

"No... I suppose not," said Blunt, considering. Then he came to a decision. "All right. I'll go out and take a look around. I'm probably not going to be able to get back to sleep anyway."

"Sorry. I'd have come out there for this one, but I'm still tied to my desk back here.... By the way, if you stop by H Division on your way, there should be a search warrant waiting for you at the front desk. I made the request in your name as soon as I got the latest news from the FBI to show probable cause."

"Right. Thanks."

"No problem. Good luck."

"Good luck, the man says," muttered Blunt after hanging up the phone. No rest for the wicked[75], *he thought, as he got up. He'd been asleep in bed, but fully dressed while he waited for the possible phone call. Now he reached for his gun and his jacket and got ready to head out and get that search warrant.*

***

At an all-night doughnut shop near the waterfront, a uniformed RCMP constable was seated at a table sipping on a cup of black coffee that he hoped would keep him awake through the rest of the graveyard shift. Chris Williams wasn't paying much attention to the few other customers in the restaurant, but his police instincts caused him to glance up and take a second look at the man that walked in the door.

The man was of average height. He was somewhat stocky in build, but moved with ease, suggesting that he wasn't in bad physical condition. He wore glasses, had greying hair cut reasonably short, and a well trimmed but greying mustache. After a quick survey of the restaurant, the man immediately walked over to the constable's table.

As Constable Williams looked up, the man removed and opened his wallet to display a badge and identification card.

"*Staff Sergeant Avery Blunt, Security Service, Counter-Intelligence,*" he said.

"*What can I do for you Staff?*' asked the constable after he'd taken a close look at the proffered ID.

"*I'm on a national security case, Williams. I need to take a quick look at some crates in a warehouse near here, and I need backup.*" He held up a hand to forestall questioning as he continued. "*Normally, I'd go through channels and arrange everything properly, but this case is breaking too quickly for that. I only recently learned where the things I'm after have been placed, and I had to use what time I had to get a search warrant. Here it is.*" He handed the warrant over for the constable's inspection.

"*I'd use your radio to call for backup, but our frequencies are being monitored. Understand?*"

"*Sure Staff,*" said the constable, barely keeping up. "*What do you want me to do?*"

"*Simple. Just follow me over to the Richmond Terminal. We'll be going to Warehouse A. That's the north one. We'll park out of sight somewhere, then I'll go in and look for the crates I'm after. All you need to do is stand at the door and make sure no one comes in to interfere while I'm in there. If I find what I think I'm going to find, I'll bring it out and then you escort me while I drive it over to headquarters. That's all. OK?*"

"*OK Staff,*" said the constable, taking a last sip of coffee and rising up.

"*Let's go then.*"

There was a large parking lot surrounding the warehouse buildings of the Richmond Terminal, but the two cars parked on the street and both men got out.

"*Do you want to just go straight in?*" asked Constable Williams.

"*Yes, but now that I've thought it over, we're going to change the plan just a bit. The doors to the warehouses are on the harbour side, so we'll walk over there. When we get there, we'll find a spot from which you can remain hidden but still watch the doors to Warehouse A. I'll go in, but you watch.*

"*Now. If a single man comes along in a bit and follows me in, let him do it but you stay put. It will be the suspect I'm after, and I'll be ready for him. If it's more than one person, then let them go, but follow them in. I'll have a better chance of dealing with them if you're there backing me up from behind. Got it?"*

"OK Staff, I've got it. What's it all about though?"

"I can't tell you that now. If everything goes according to plan and I can wrap this thing up tonight, then I'll be able to tell you later because secrecy won't matter any more at that point. That's the best I can do.... Ready?"

"Ready."

"Let's move. Keep your eyes open"

Constable Williams was fully awake now, as the two men walked across the parking lot, taking some care to avoid walking in the better lit portions that surrounded the several lamp-posts on the lot. When they reached the harbour side, it was easy to find a stack of empty pallets, behind which the constable took-up station.

"How long do you think you'll be in there?" asked Williams.

"If I'm right, and the crates I'm looking for are in there, then an hour. Two hours at the most. If I'm wrong, then we'll have to stake the place out until dawn. After that I'll use your car radio to get another team out here to relieve us."

"OK Staff. Good luck."

***

Everything seemed quiet as Staff Sergeant Blunt walked cautiously to the main double-doors on the harbour-facing side of Warehouse A. It's quiet... too quiet, *he thought, grimly, remembering the trite line used in so many old Western and war movies. Reaching the doors, he withdrew a slim case containing lock-picking tools, took a good look at the deadbolt lock and selected a pair of picks. Working with one pick in each hand, he used a very slender one to pick each pin in succession, and an L-shaped tension wrench to hold the picked pins in place. Once he had successfully picked all of the pins, he used the tension wrench to turn the key-cylinder and open the lock.*

Blunt quietly opened the door and went in, closing the door behind him. Gazing around, he could see that only about half of the warehouse lights were turned on, providing just enough illumination for a person to be able to navigate around the cavernous space. His rubber-soled shoes enabled him to move very quietly as he chose an indirect route to the northeast corner of the building. As he approached the indicated corner, he couldn't hear anything but there was one location from which a bit more light was emanating. Slowing down, and watching and listening even more carefully – if that was possible – he approached the light.

As he rounded the corner of a stack of crates, he found the source of the additional light. A 12V, 'Big Jim' style hand lantern was sitting on top of a large crate, with its swivel-head lamp aimed towards the cement floor where several crates had been pulled down and opened. One of the opened crates revealed two shiny projectiles of the kind that might be fired from a large cannon. Like howitzer projectiles, *he thought. Approaching the crate, and kneeling down for a better look, he could see some unusual features: each projectile had a gleaming casing that might have been stainless-steel or brushed aluminum, and an odd-looking access hatch of some kind near the base. There was also a small, black-plastic box that appeared to be a remote control. In the upper half of the face, there was a small red indicator light and a large, oblong, grey push-button switch. The red light was on.*

He only had time to frown, before he felt a sharp pain in the side of his neck, a cloth bag came over his head, and he was thrown to the floor.

Although Blunt struggled, he was disoriented by the bag which made it almost impossible to breathe, and his attacker had the advantage of being on top of him. As the seconds went by, he not only couldn't breathe but became quite dizzy, making his struggles weaker and weaker.

Drugged, *he thought, as he lost consciousness.*

His assailant knelt and crouched overhead, positioning Blunt's arms so he could handcuff him.

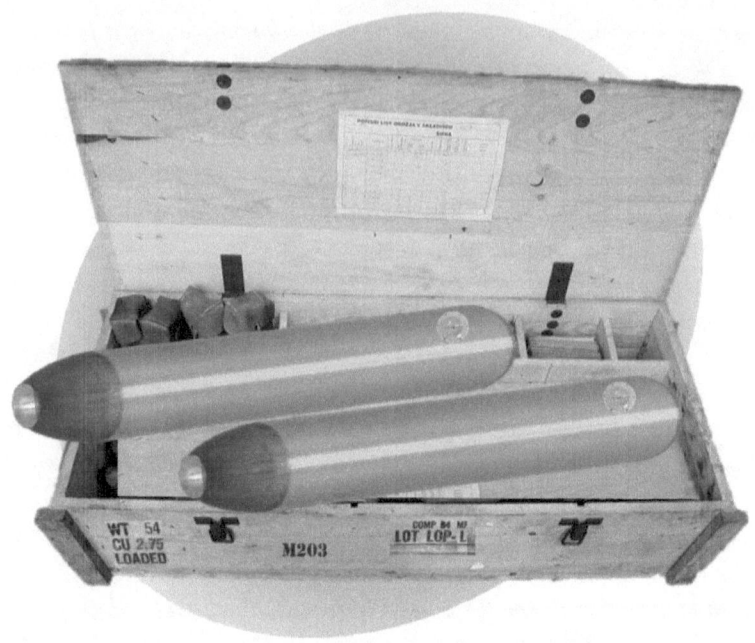

The Modified M549 Rocket-Assist Projectile

"I think that's enough Bob," I said as I emerged, with Silver by my side, from my place of concealment behind a stack of crates. At the sound of my voice, Jack emerged from another stack a few metres to one side, and Vivian did the same from a stack that was a few metres to the other side of me.

Bob, who had frozen in-place at the sound of my voice, slowly rose from his crouch over Avery and turned. As he did so, I gasped. It was Avery, but then it wasn't either. The man facing me either wore a wig or had his hair dyed to match Avery's greying dark brown. His eyebrows had been similarly treated or attached, as was the moustache. Bob, however, had blonde hair and was clean shaven. Despite the glasses, I could see that he wore contact lenses to change his apparent eye colour from blue to brown. Although Bob was quite slender, the figure before me wore padding, or possibly layers of clothing, to give the appearance of a more heavyset build. He'd also done something to darken his skin tone, and must have put padding in each cheek. The voice, however, was unmistakably Bob's.

"I'm impressed, Bob. Except for the voice, I'd probably pass you on the street without recognition."

He shrugged. "Tradecraft," was all he said.

"The real Avery. Is he OK or did you kill him?"

"No, he'll be fine. I used a fast-acting anesthetic, and choked him a bit to give it time to take effect, but he was breathing freely when I put the cuffs on him." He stepped aside so I could see and, sure enough, Avery's wrists were handcuffed together.

"You were a bit rough on him, don't you think?"

"Well, I was all alone here so I had to make sure I could arrest him. He was armed. See?" Bob lifted a snub-nose revolver, using his thumb and forefinger to hold it handgrip up, with the barrel pointing down towards the floor.

"I only just found out that he was the traitor everyone's been looking for all these years, so I had to get the jump on him right away. There was no time to call it in."

"How did you find him out?" It was amazing to me that I could carry on this conversation in a normal pace and tone of voice.

"Simple," he smiled. "I had suspected him all along, just like the FBI did." He nodded towards Vivian. "When I told him that I wasn't able to come out from Ottawa in time, he agreed to do it. It was our office that made all the travel arrangements for him, including his hotel reservation." Bob shrugged. "Once I knew that I was able to call the hotel and request a specific room. Then I had his phone tapped."

"Legally?"

He looked at me like I was stupid. "Of course I didn't do it legally. In this case, I thought the ends justified the means. When Avery here shows up in court – if it ever comes to court, that is – I think the judge will overlook such a minor transgression in this particular case. Don't you?"

I sighed. "I suppose so. Except for one thing. The traitor wasn't Avery, Bob. It was you. All along the way, it was you."

"You're crazy Alex!" Bob exclaimed. "Or maybe...." His tone changed to conciliatory. "Maybe you've been working too hard lately. Maybe you need to take a bit of leave and rest up."

Nice try, I thought.

"You might be right, Bob. But one thing I'm sure of is the

identity of our traitor. Think back for a moment. Way back. All the way back 20 years, to the Avro Arrow incident. Our leak offered to sell the Arrow secrets to the British, and actually pulled it off over a complicated series of dead drops in which packages of documents were dropped off in return for envelopes of money. Naturally the British were keen to find out who their mysterious benefactor was. They tried, but they failed. As it turns out, they actually did get the evidence they needed, but they hadn't known what to look for, so they never even knew what they had."

"What do you mean, evidence?"

"Well, every time you set up a dead drop, they had operatives rush over and set up surveillance. At least, such surveillance as they could position on short notice. Since you tended to use crowded locations, they never actually spotted you pick up the money, but they took a huge number of photographs hoping to spot something in the crowds. As I said, though, it didn't do them any good."

"What's your evidence then?"

"Well. Surprise number one, is that they kept all those pictures, and then at some point in time they sent them home to be stored in the MI6 archives. Surprise number two, is that they're still there collecting dust after all these years. Surprise number three, is that I visited MI6 and they let me in to see those pictures, and I went through them too. They took thousands of them, and if you looked at them all there were several hundred people whose faces you could make out in some of them. And that's what I did. I went through every one looking to see if I could spot a familiar face. You see what I had, that MI6 didn't, was a knowledge of the twenty suspects and what each of them look like."

Bob didn't comment, but the look on his face made it clear that he knew what was coming next.

"Surprise number four was that I spotted one familiar face, Bob. It was yours. You were younger then, but it was you."

"Damn them! They promised not to try to identify me as part of the deal to get the documents."

"Yes. I'm afraid that spies tend to lie when it suits them. Surprising, huh?"

Bob growled, low in his throat, and surveyed our positions. Then, changing his grip, he pointed Avery's revolver at me.

As my revolver was already in my hand, I was able to point it at

Bob at the same time.

"Standoff, Bob," I said.

"Not quite," he responded. With his other hand, he had reached into a pocket and he pulled out the remote-control device, holding it so we could see that the red light was on.

"Just tell me this, Bob. Why? Why betray everyone so many times, through so many years?" I didn't think he'd actually tell me, but he did.

"As I've told you before Alex, it's all just a game, really. Not at first. At first, we were all on a mission; a crusade; good versus evil, and all that. Then, later, it became somewhat of a game. A game for competitive people. Naturally, some play it better than others, and eventually you begin to wonder: Who's the best? And then you wonder: How would you even know? Eventually, the game became more important than the job, and I realized that the winner is really just the person that can fool most of the people, most of the time[76]."

"OK, but think, Bob!" I pleaded. "What comes now? If you shoot one of us, the others will come at you, and you must know how fast Silver can be."

Bob tilted his head as Silver had already begun to growl and silently begin a flanking maneuver.

"Tell him to stop, or I'll shoot Vivian," he said, in a very calm, serious voice. I believed him.

I told Silver to stop.

"Even if you manage to get all of us, the place is surrounded. You won't get past the dockyard."

"Nice try," he responded. "That's one of the oldest bluffs in the books."

I shrugged. "I'm actually telling the truth. I do that, you know. But, suit yourself. I've warned you. What happens next is on your head."

Thinking furiously, I saw Bob's eyes grow cunning as he decided on his next move. Keeping Avery's revolver pointed at me, he picked up one of the shiny projectiles and tucked it under his arm, behind his gun hand. "See this projectile? Just before Avery came in, I opened the access panel at its base and switched on the remote triggering device."

Next, he held up the little black box in his free hand. "And this is the remote control. You can see that it's live. The FBI was kind enough to send the instructions in case we had to turn it off. I turned it on instead.

"That makes it a 'Non-Zero-Sum Game.' If I lose, you all lose – our lives, in this case. Now then," he was back to feeling like he was in charge. "If you'll just step aside, I'll just take this remote control and walk out of here. Then I'll toss it away, leave the country, and never come back."

"Bob. Please," I tried once more. "The place really is surrounded – by MPs – and they're going to be inclined to shoot first and ask questions later. And even if you get by them, the CIA's going to be on your trail wherever you go. In fact, I wouldn't be at all surprised if there's a CIA agent waiting outside right now."

"You're bluffing again, Alex. You're a good chess player, but you're not yet in my league… and, even if you're right, I'm willing to take my chances."

I sighed, theatrically. "OK Bob, but just put the projectile and the remote control back in the crate. If you do, you can walk out of here. But you should know that, if I have to, I'll take you down to prevent you from stealing that weapon."

Bob had begun to take a step forward, but now he stopped and looked at me quizzically, with his head tilted to one side. "You'll take me down? Me? After all we've been through together?" he asked.

I shrugged. "I could ask you the very same question. Think Bob? Please! Leave the projectile behind and you can live."

"Silver! Stay!" I ordered. With my peripheral vision, I could tell that Silver, his senses on high, was positioning himself to spring towards Bob, aiming for his gun hand. Unfortunately, Silver was not in position to have been able to get at the gun in time, so I didn't want to take the risk of making the situation worse.

There was dead silence in the warehouse for a moment. Then, several things happened almost simultaneously.

Bob made his decision. He glanced at Silver, but kept his gun aimed at me and began to squeeze the trigger.

Vivian, screamed "He's going to shoot!" but she was too far away to physically interfere.

Jack didn't say a thing, but had begun to move. By the time I realized what he planned, it was too late. With a tremendous leap, he sprung right in front of me, just as Bob pulled the trigger.

The sound of a .38 Special round being fired in a confined space is unforgettable. Even in a firing range, while wearing hearing protection, it's loud. But for our unprotected ears, it was painful and dangerous; louder than a jet plane taking off; louder than a jackhammer.

The force of the slug drove Jack back into me, causing me to drop to the floor with Jack in my lap as I struggled to keep my gun lined-up on Bob. I'd been hoping to create an opportunity to use the anesthetic-dart-shooting pen that Emi had given me, but it was far too late for that now.

I don't know whether Bob had ever shot anyone before. Unlike me, many police officers go their entire careers with having to draw their gun, much less fire it in a dangerous situation. Whatever the reason, he froze for a moment, as if taking in the fact that he'd actually shot a fellow officer and the spy game was now more than an academic exercise. All I know is that in the instant it took for him to regained control of himself, I'd pointed my revolver straight at his heart.

Silver, worried by the distress he sensed in me and torn between my command to stay put and the danger he sensed in Bob, stayed where he was, vibrating, still growling, and poised to leap at a command from me.

"If I have to, I'll shoot you too," said Bob, but I could tell he realized that he had run out of options.

"It's still a standoff, Bob, and those sounds…" We could all hear the warehouse doors burst open, and the sound of running boots. "Those sounds are from MPs; the reinforcements you didn't believe me about."

I was distracted for a moment by Jack, who suddenly began to move around, which caused him to start coughing up blood. I couldn't even take the time yet to figure out where he had been shot because I had to keep my eyes on Bob. Silver was waiting for a command from me. Vivian, who was unarmed, had to stand her ground and wait. And me? For a moment, I suddenly felt separated from reality.

Time slowed down, and it was like I was detached from the current reality and was watching a scene from a movie, from outside my body even. Like a spectator.

Jack lay dying in my arms.

I saw myself looking angrily at Bob, with my gun pointed straight at his chest; my finger on the trigger; and tears streaming down my face.

I saw Silver stand nearby, looking so confused because for the first time in all the years we'd been together he didn't know what to do.

I heard Bob snarl: "Finish it, Alex. It's all over for me now anyway. You know you want to do it. Pull the trigger and get it over with."

I was distressed and angry, and I found that I wanted to do it. My finger began a well practised maneuver: a very slow, gradual squeeze.

Then, I seemed to hear another voice. It was a quiet but compelling voice. I don't even know why I could hear it with everything else going on, but somehow it penetrated through the mental fog, and I found myself angling my head, trying to make out the words.

"You can lower the gun now, Alex. We have him covered." Such a gentle, yet persuasive sound. "This isn't the Mountie's way. Your way.... Take a breath and let it go."

It was Don's voice. Was he finally here? I see myself risk a quick glance to one side. Yes, definitely Don, dressed as an MP Captain and pointing his own gun at Bob. A large, angry-looking .45 automatic. There are others with him.

Could it really be over at last?

"Let it go Alex..." I hear again. So softly.

Suddenly, I hear Bob snarl and point the gun at his own head instead. There is another deafening crack. The sound acts like a jolt, like when a film projector skips a sprocket, almost jams, and then gets realigned and carries on. Suddenly I'm back in real time. In my own body.

I see Bob drop his gun and collapse to the floor. I look dumbly at my revolver, ease my finger back, and lower the gun. I can feel that Silver has come over to rest his head on my leg. He gives a moan of sympathy.

That's when the shakes began.

Laurie Schramm

8 AFTERMATH

With reinforcements having finally arrived, plus a bewildered-looking Constable Williams, several tasks were quickly delegated.

Don detailed one of his MPs to radio-in for paramedics and to see if they could get a Navy helicopter in fast for a medivac to one of the big hospitals.

Vivian helped me to find and apply pressure to the holes in Jack's body. Bob's bullet had gone right through and, if it hadn't hit the heart, it certainly hit a major artery as both holes were bleeding like crazy. Jack was still coughing, but he'd lost consciousness.

Other MPs went to attend to Avery, who was still alive and had regained consciousness during the standoff. With his hands handcuffed, however, he hadn't been able to do much more than pull the black bag off of his head. The bag, incidentally, turned out to be constructed from black cloth that had been coated on the inside with some kind of extremely flexible and clingy plastic. That was why Bob had been able to so quickly restrict Avery's breathing, allowing him to be overpowered long enough for the fast-acting anesthetic to take effect.

Meanwhile, Don came up to ask Vivian and I some urgent questions.

"Are you OK?" he asked me, putting a comforting hand on my shoulder.

"No. But I'm not injured, if that's what you mean."

"Those projectiles. Is there any risk of them going off?" was his second question. "When Bob dropped the one that he was holding, my heart stopped for a moment."

It was probably the stress of the situation, but that sent Vivian into almost hysterical laughter. Unable to speak for a moment, she waved in my direction.

"No, it's OK Don." I said, tiredly. "The CIA made them up for the FBI, at my request. They resemble something the CIA is actually working on, but these ones are just fakes."

"Nobody tells me anything," Don complained. "So, it was all part of a sting then? A ruse?"

"A complete fabrication, from beginning to end. It had to be tempting enough to be useful as bait, and Bob thought he was going to be able to sell these new projectiles on the black market. It was also designed to provide Bob with an opportunity to frame Avery, so he'd take the fall for everything. We'd never have been able to pull it off without the help of the FBI and the CIA."

"And it worked!"

"Well, sort of, but at what cost?" I said, crying again. "God what a mess!"

As luck would have it, the navy had a helicopter airborne in the harbour area, and it was diverted to the huge dock outside the warehouse, which made a perfect landing platform, even for the huge Sikorsky. It was carrying a Search and Rescue Technician, who quickly examined Jack and got him hustled into the helicopter, which immediately took off with a deafening roar and headed for one of the big hospitals downtown.

When the paramedic ambulance showed up, Avery allowed himself to be examined but refused to be taken to hospital. He was amazed at the degree to which Bob had been able to replicate his appearance. He was wearing baggy pants, and a kind of padded vest under an oversize coat, to mimic Avery's heftier build. He'd dyed his blonde hair and eyebrows brown and added streaks of grey. He'd glued on a false moustache and heavier eyebrows, similarly coloured and streaked. He'd dyed his naturally pale face, neck, and hands just slightly to better match Avery's skin tone, and more.

"He's wearing contact lenses to change his eye colour," said Avery, inspecting the body closely. "And he's got pads in his cheeks to puff out his face."

I came over to see for myself, and glanced at the fake ID that Avery had retrieved from Bob's wallet. "Not bad. Wouldn't survive a close inspection, but from a medium distance it looks pretty good, and that's all he needed."

The paramedics took Bob's body away, and Don's MPs gathered up the crate and the two fake projectiles. It was just after dawn by the time we were walking out of the warehouse, and in the early morning light we noticed that we were being watched by someone who was sitting on a bench by the waterfront edge of the dock.

"Company?" I murmured.

Vivian followed my gaze, then did a double-take and said: "You do have a way with words, sometimes, Alex. Wait here, please."

As Vivian walked over to the bench, the figure rose. It was an elderly-looking man; medium height and build. He had scraggly, grey hair sticking out at odd angles from under a tired-looking hat, and wore a shabby-looking grey sport-coat with baggy pants. In one hand, he seemed to be clutching a rumpled brown paper bag of the sort that a suspicious-minded person might guess held a whiskey bottle. He stood hunched over when Vivian began speaking to him but, near the end, he straightened up and I was surprised to see that he was actually quite tall.

After a brief conversation, they shook hands, and Vivian walked back to rejoin us.

"Let me guess, CIA?" I said.

"CIA. They don't care about the dummy projectiles. In fact, he said we were welcome to keep them as souvenirs. What they *were* interested in was the identity of the traitor, and they sent him to observe."

"That and to make sure that we actually caught the right person?"

"They'd never admit that, but I wouldn't be at all surprised," said Vivian, with a smile.

"By the way," said Avery, "you didn't tell me the CIA projectiles were fake."

"No. Sorry about that. It was the same reason I didn't tell you that Bob was Gideon. I wanted to make sure your reactions were real when things unfolded. I am sorry you had such a close call with Bob, though."

"That's OK Alex. It was worth it to find the real traitor and to get my name cleared once and for all."

"While we're discussing your little surprises," Vivian chimed in. "Where did that remote control business come from? It wasn't the CIA. That access panel was supposed to be the way to set codes and a timer for the thing."

"I know, but I had a colleague put an addendum on your message with the arming instructions. Then, I slipped the remote into the crate when we were first selecting our hiding places in here. I thought we might need to stall for time because there would be no way to know how close Don and his MPs would be in the critical moments and I thought it might be handy to be able to make Bob think he had the upper hand for a while. It didn't work out as well as I'd hoped though. Which reminds me," I said, digging in my shirt pocket. "Here you are Don. It's actually the remote control for your garage door opener."

Even though the mission had succeeded, it had been a horrible day for me, and it got worse a few hours later when we learned the awful news that Jack had been pronounced 'Dead on Arrival' when the helicopter reached the hospital. It's always shocking when you learn that a colleague has died, at any age, and it made me feel worse that he died in my arms, and guilty that he'd died in his heroic move to save my life. He'd been a good colleague and friend. Silver and I attended his funeral later on, as did many other police officers from across Canada. Don came out for it, in full military dress uniform, and even Vivian flew back up to Canada for it.

Jack's buried at the RCMP Cemetery at Depot Division, Regina, where he and I had first met as fellow recruits in training. It's a peaceful place. Silver and I still go and visit him there when we're in Regina.

Stained-Glass Windows in the RCMP Chapel,
Depot Division, Regina

Laurie Schramm

9 EPILOGUE

Early November, 1981
Ottawa, ON

I thought I'd be sent on leave after my debriefing in Ottawa, to give me time to grieve and wind-down from everything that had happened, but no.

Staff Sergeant Avery Blunt was made acting Head of Section and, presumably on the orders of Uncle George, had taken some pains to make sure I was constantly being sent out on assignments, including assignments that would never have come to our section, or even the Security Service for that matter. They weren't exactly traffic duty, but it was obvious that they were trying to keep me busy and occupy my mind with current work as much as possible. I think they were just trying to be kind, and I can't say that they were wrong.

I thought I'd heard the last of what became known as the Gideon Case, but I was wrong about that too. It came up again one day in the third week of November. Silver and I were returning to Ottawa from a search for a missing child. The child had been found, unharmed, by one of the other search parties, but the important thing was that it all ended well, so I was feeling quite content when my police radio crackled and the dispatcher relayed a message that I was to proceed to a certain address and meet the officer on the scene.

I mustn't have fully had my wits about me as I remember

thinking that it was interesting to be called to a house in the Rockcliffe Park area because that's where the Gideon Case had all begun for me – at Deputy Commissioner George MacLeod's house party. I hadn't remembered Uncle George's address, but it all came back to me when I realized that it was his house to which I'd been called.

Standing on the front step of the house was Uncle George himself, the 'officer on the scene.' As Silver and I walked up the sidewalk to the front steps, I could see that Uncle George's wife, Mary MacLeod was standing there as well. Having saluted Uncle George and been hugged by Mary, we were invited in.

"I hope you don't mind being summoned like you were, but an opportunity came up on such short notice that there wasn't time for an informal invitation."

"It's no problem, Sir. We were returning from a child-search anyway. I'm just sorry that every time I come here, I seem to be wearing a soiled uniform."

He laughed. "Don't worry about that. If anything, it reflects the way you always seem to be on the job, getting things done."

"Did you find the lost child, dear?" asked Mary.

I smiled. "Well, Silver and I didn't, but another of the search teams did so it had a happy ending. That's the important thing."

Once I'd slipped my boots off, I was invited to join Uncle George in his study, just like I had been almost exactly a year earlier. As if he'd read my mind, Uncle George echoed the same sentiment.

"Ever watch the old *Mission: Impossible*[77] series on television?" he asked, as we walked through the house.

"Yes Sir. I used to watch them with my father every week. We almost never missed an episode."

"I enjoyed them too, never thinking that one day I'd be assigning an impossible mission to someone, but that's what I did almost exactly one year ago in this very room."

"He refused to bet on the outcome, too," said the familiar voice of Admiral White.

"It's great to see you again, Sir!" I said, walking over to shake his hand, followed by Silver who walked over, gave the Admiral a good sniffing over, then decided he recognized him and went to lie down on a rug.

"I'm sorry about Constable McDonald," said Uncle George, as

we all found comfortable chairs to sink into.

"Me too, Sir. He was great colleague and a good friend, and he deliberately threw himself in front of a bullet that Bob meant for me. I'll never forget him."

"Good. There are two things you can do for him now. Honour his memory and keep moving. I'm sure that's what he would have wanted."

I nodded. I agreed.

"Well then. I want to talk to you briefly about what people are now calling the Gideon Case. I read the report of your debriefing, of course, and I've spoken with Staff Sergeant Blunt and Deputy Director Wheeler in Washington. I didn't call you in right away because I wanted to give you some time to decompress and work through some of the grieving. You can blame me for making Blunt keep you busy with assignments, but I thought it might help you to be occupied."

"Thank you, Sir. I think it was the best thing to do."

"And you're feeling OK now?"

"Mostly Sir. I think," I hedged.

"Well, I won't pry any further. Now then, we'd like to hear about it in your own words, if you don't mind."

So, I told them my story, briefly, but holding nothing of any significance back.

"Amazing," said Uncle George. "A fine job. Well, congratulations on pulling off an impossible mission. You succeeded where everyone else failed. Admiral White here offered to bet a case of Scotch that'd you'd crack the case, but I wouldn't take it because I thought you'd pull it off as well. The few others that were in the know: Deputy Director Wheeler, his counterpart at the CIA, and 'C' at MI6 all thought it was a lost cause, that the traitor had covered his tracks too well, but they were wrong. They're all very impressed with you now though, I can tell you."

"Thank you, Sirs, both of you. I was very fortunate."

"Certainly, but you made your own luck. Took a few unconventional leaps while you were at it too. But they paid off."

"How did you ever get me into MI6 Sir? And how did you manage to get the CIA to play along?"

"As far as MI6 goes, that was Admiral White's doing, but our two nations' military intelligence services have a long history of helping each other out. Almost as long as the Mounted Police's relationship with the FBI, in fact."

"Once I explained everything to C," the admiral put in, "he was almost as eager as we were to get the matter solved."

"As for the CIA," continued Uncle George, "I can't take much credit there either. I just asked Director Wheeler to give it his best shot. I don't know how he did it, but Director Wheeler must have done some fast talking to get the CIA to play along."

"Well, it would all have been for nothing without their help. I just wish it hadn't turned out to be Bob that was the traitor Gideon. I knew I had to treat Bob like all the other suspects, but I really didn't want it to be him."

"You would rather it had turned out to be someone like Demeniak in A Section, hmmm?" He immediately threw a hand up. "No! Don't answer that. I shouldn't have said that out loud."

He saw the look on my face though, as I realized that I hadn't been entirely successful in preventing the corners of my mouth from curling up in a repressed smile.

"I suspect our thoughts are running on similar lines, but you did not hear me say that!"

"No, Sir. Of course not."

"Well, like you, I knew Bob had to be a possibility, but I didn't want it to be him either. He joined up when he turned 18 and had nearly twenty-five years in the Force. He would have been getting his fifth star[78] later this year. Back in 1959, he was a constable in the Security and Intelligence Directorate[79], the forerunner of the Security Service. The problem was that none of us suspected him any more or any less than the other 19 on the list."

"He was very good at his job, Sir, it's just that he turned those same skills and abilities against us."

"Yes," said Admiral White. "It's the old story of 'who watches the watchers?'"

"True, but it was worse than that," added Uncle George. "Ever since the 1950s and '60s, the intelligence thinking has been that there must be at least one traitor within, and a lot of effort was poured into trying to discover who it was. This was going on in intelligence agencies all around the world, including ours[80].

"Furthermore, the counter-intelligence thinking has tended to focus on the ideologically-motivated traitor, leading counter-intelligence officers – including ours - to overlook the threat from betrayals based on non-ideological motives and chase innocent, or even mythical, people. In Bob's case, it wasn't ideology, it was the challenge, and the money."

"And 'the game' Sir. I think the money was more like a way of keeping score. He was certainly too smart to spend it and be caught living an extravagant lifestyle."

"There, you see? 'The Game' became more important to him than the reason the game exists in the first place. That's why we needed someone – you, in fact - to take a fresh approach; be unconventional. Incidentally, what was the most difficult part of the case for you?" asked Uncle George, changing the subject.

"It was after I recognized Bob at one of the dead drops in two of the MI6 photos. When I came back to the office, I did my best not to reveal any hint of what I'd learned, especially to Bob himself. But the whole time I was afraid I would give out some kind of tiny sign and the jig would be up. Luckily for me, the look on Bob's face when I confronted him in Halifax showed that he'd had no idea. None at all."

"And then you set a trap for him. A huge trap."

"I'm just glad it worked. A lot more things could have gone wrong than actually did."

"Well. It's a huge relief to everyone who's in the know that you succeeded in closing off the leak, and Admiral White and I wanted to express our appreciation in person. Thank you."

"Thank you from me too," said the Admiral. "By the way, what did you think of your brief career as a Captain in the RCAF?"

"At first, it all seemed so bizarre, especially the part about being saluted. But later, once I was deep inside the role I was playing, it became kind of fun."

"Good," he said with a smile. "I hear that you impressed Lieutenant Moore and Sergeant Wilson."

"The feeling's mutual, Sir. I'd work with them again anytime."

"Well now," said Uncle George, bringing the meeting back to order. "The reason for calling you in here without notice was that the Admiral just flew in for another meeting today, and has to fly out again later tonight, so this was our window of opportunity. The two of us wanted to see you in person and together to offer our thanks… and our congratulations" His eyes twinkled.

"Congratulations, Sir?"

"Yes. You've just been promoted to Sergeant."

"Congratulations, Sergeant Houston," they both said, almost in unison. Mary, who'd been silent to this point, simply got up and came over to give me a big hug before the two men could approach and shake hands.

"Thank you, Sirs," I said. "But...."

"Just doing your job? Don't expect prizes or rewards? Hmmm?" said the Admiral.

"Something like that," was the best I could come up with.

"Well. It's not a prize. I suppose is a bit of a reward, to some extent. It's not everyday someone catches a traitor from within. But, at the same time, it's not specifically for the Gideon Case. More like for that and all the other cases of yours that came before it. Here's the promotion notice. It's effective today, so make sure your trip home is the last one you take wearing corporal's stripes."

I thanked him again.

"I also have a copy of a letter here that I'd like you to read later on," he continued. "It's the letter of recommendation for your promotion. It's rather lengthy, and it's signed by me, the Admiral here, Deputy Director White, and 'C' of MI6. You're not supposed to have it, so I'm not really giving you a copy, you understand."

"Yes, Sir. Thank you, Sir."

"Fine. As long as we're breaking rules, I think we should have one drink to celebrate, and then the Admiral's driver should be here to take him to the airport."

Later, as we walked from Uncle George's house to our truck, I looked down at Silver and said: "What do you think about it all, Silver?"

He looked up at me with his head tilted to one side, showing that he was paying attention and attempting to discern the gist of my words.

There was definitely a cross roads approaching. I was becoming too well known in too many places to continue doing much more undercover work, especially in anything involving foreign agents. At the same time, the Security Service had come under a huge storm of public controversy due its actions during the 1970 FLQ crisis[81]. In August, the McDonald Commission had recommended that the service be split-out from the Mounted Police and rebuilt as a civilian intelligence agency, thus separating policing and intelligence work into separate organizations. When the time came,

I was pretty sure I was going to have to leave the Security Service in order to remain with the Mounted Police. My career goal had been policing, and none of my experiences in ten years as a police officer had changed that.

I knelt down on the sidewalk and looked Silver straight in the eyes.

"What should we do Silver?" I asked.

As he stared back at me with that mesmerizing gaze that he seemed to be able to turn on or off at will, an image floated into my consciousness.

I saw a First Nations human and a wild-looking wolf. It was a drawing of the first human-and-wolf bonding from ancient times, and I remembered that an elder in Skagway, Alaska had shown me that image. The elder that had originally instructed Silver and his sister when they were young. The elder had explained that, in the legend of their nation, the first human-wolf pair had become famous for noble deeds involving justice and the protection of the weak and the disadvantaged.

The next image, or sense perhaps, that entered my mind contained the words *We are pack*.

Throwing my arms around Silver's shoulders in a big hug, I nodded my head and said: "Pack."

"*Grruph*," said Silver, sounding satisfied.

It was enough. When the time came, we'd figure something out, together.

... Alex and Silver will return,
in *"An Interrupted Mountie."*

Laurie Schramm

SUMMARY

RCMP Corporal Alexandra Houston is drawn further into the shadowy world of espionage and betrayal when she is asked to hunt for a security leak that is buried somewhere inside one of Canada's intelligence services. But which one? If it's within her own service, the 'leak' may already be aware of her assignment, in which case the hunter could become the hunted.

Laurie Schramm

ABOUT THE AUTHOR

Laurie Schramm comes from an RCMP family, grew up while living in the RCMP Barracks (Depot Division) in Regina, Saskatchewan, and spent several summers working as a civilian for the RCMP while in high school and university. Early personal influences included not only the real-life RCMP culture but also Hollywood's versions via such classics as *Rose Marie*, and *Susannah of the Mounties*. Many of the events described in this novel are based on the author's real life, although not necessarily within an RCMP context.

For more information, see Laurier L. Schramm on **Linked** in

and:

www.laurieschramm.ca

or

www.facebook.com/LaurieSchrammBooks

Laurie Schramm

ENDNOTES

1. Adapted from the CIA's 'Moscow Rules." See A.J. Mendez and J. Mendez, *"The Moscow Rules: The Secret CIA Tactics That Helped America Win the Cold War,"* PublicAffairs, N.Y., 2019. The 'Murphy's Law' adage may have originated from mathematician Augustus De Morgan, who in 1866 wrote: *"whatever can happen will happen."* In modern usage, it generally means: *"Anything that can go wrong, will go wrong."*
2. From the 1854 poem *The Charge of the Light Brigade*, by Alfred, Lord Tennyson.
3. Hansard, "Announcement of Government Policy on Air Defence," House of Commons Debates, Official Report, Ottawa, ON, Friday, February 20, 1959.
4. With the passage of time, and the declassification and release of increasing amounts of formerly secret material, it appears that a number of factors were at play. Budget was a consideration, as air defence was consuming a large portion of Canada's military budget, and this included not only the Arrow program but also the Boeing Michigan Aeronautical Research Center missile program (BOMARC; an anti-missile missile), and the semi-automated ground environment program (SAGE; an air defence system that included radars, computers, and direction centres). The Americans, for their part, had a number of reasons for possibly not wanting Canada to build the Arrow,

among which was anticipation that it would be the only aircraft in the world capable of the detecting and intercepting the CIA's U-2 spy planes (which they publicly insisted were weather-research aircraft).

5. See P. Campagna, *"Storms of Controversy: The Secret Avro Arrow Files Revealed,"* 4th Ed., Dundurn Press, Toronto, 2010.

6. The Department of Defence Production recorded three of the completed aircraft, and the one partially completed aircraft, as having been destroyed by July 7, 1959. Two more were recorded to be in the process of dismantlement, with expected completion within the same month. There seems to be some lack of clarity about the fate of the fifth completed Arrow, leading to speculation that it was spirited away and may still exist – somewhere. See endnote 5.

7. Although mechanical paper-shredding machines have been manufactured since the mid-1930s, they were used almost exclusively by governments until the mid-1980s, and were only more recently adopted into business and home use.

8. In the Security Service, at this time in history, B Section dealt with counter-espionage. See: J. Sawatsky, *"Men in the Shadows. The RCMP Security Service,"* Doubleday, Toronto, 1980.

9. At various times, in fact, several countries quietly expressed interested in the Arrow and/or its Iroquois engines, including France, the U.K., and the U.S.

10. In 1959, many hospitals were still refusing to allow fathers-to-be to go in past Admitting with their partners-in-labour. By the 1960s, most hospitals had begun to allow fathers into the delivery room during labour, and by the 1970s some were being allowed to remain for the actual birth.

11. A collection of documents produced by Avro Canada, subcontractors and the National Aeronautical Establishment are held in the archives of Canada's National Science Library. Among these are nearly 600 declassified documents that are available to the public. See: Avro Canada CF-105 Arrow Collection, National Science Library, National Research Council of Canada, Ottawa, ON.

12. A common term used to refer to a member of an intelligence service. Depending on the context, this could mean someone from the same country or someone from an allied country.

13. In real life, a complete set of blueprints did survive, having

been taken home and hidden by one of the senior draftsmen on the project. CBC News announced their existence in 2020, and they were put on display at the Diefenbaker Centre at the University of Saskatchewan between January and April of that year. See: D. Shield, "Avro Arrow blueprints on display...." CBC News, January 6, 2020. https://www.cbc.ca/news/canada/saskatoon/saved-avro-arrow-blueprints-ordered-destroyed-1.5416554.

14. A dead drop is any secret location that can be used to pass messages, documents, or other objects between two people without the need to ever meet face-to-face. The locations can be changed as often as desired, and a variety of methods can be used to signal when a drop has been made.

15. Ontario Provincial Police.

16. See: J. Starnes, *"Closely Guarded: A Life in Canadian Security and Intelligence,"* University of Toronto Press, Toronto, 1998.

17. Non-commissioned officers.

18. Joe Clark led the Progressive Conservate Party of Canada in three general elections, served one term as Prime Minister (1979-80) and two as Leader of the Official Opposition in the House of Commons (1976-79 and 1980-83).

19. Heavy water meaning water composed of deuterium and oxygen atoms rather than hydrogen and oxygen atoms. CANDU meaning CANadian Deuterium Uranium nuclear reactor systems, which use natural (not enriched) uranium fuel, moderated by heavy water.

20. Atomic Energy of Canada Limited, a federal Crown Corporation and the developer of the CANDU reactor technology.

21. In real life, Canadian passports were in high demand for Soviet espionage operations during the Cold War. The detection of fraudulent passport applications was made difficult when legitimate documents were obtained by people using faked identities. Post-second-world-war Canada was experiencing massive immigration, under cover of which illegal immigrants could, if they were patient enough, "assume the identities of deceased Canadians, acquire social insurance and Medicare numbers, establish work records, pay taxes, draw on social benefits, and so on, thus gradually filling out a profile that would be very hard to detect as false." See: R. Whitaker, G.S.

Kealey, and A. Parnaby, *"Secret Service. Political Policing in Canada from the Fenians to Fortress America,"* University of Toronto Press, Toronto, 2012.

22. In real life, the RCMP did attempt to uncover a suspected Soviet mole during the Cold War. The operation was called Feather Bed, and stretched from the late 1950s to the 1970s, but there seems to be no public evidence it ever identified the mole, who was later identified by a Soviet defector (in 1985). See: J. Bronskill, "RCMP's Fruitless Cold War Mole Hunt Included Senior Diplomats Ignatieff and Rae, Archives Show," *Toronto Star*, 22 March 2012.

23. See *An Indestructible Mountie* (ISBN: 978-1-9994940-4-9).

24. See *An Inseparable Mountie* (ISBN: 978-1-7772424-0-4).

25. See *An Intrepid Mountie* (ISBN: 978-1-7772424-6-6).

26. Counter-espionage. See endnote #8.

27. STU-I was the first of a series of digital, Secure Telephone Units (STUs) developed for the U.S. National Security Agency in the 1970s. The desktop telephone part looked much like a regular telephone, but it was connected to a sizeable cabinet containing racks of electronics. Subsequent generations, STU-II and STU-III were developed in the 1980s that approached the goal of a true desktop unit.

28. See *An Ineradicable Mountie* (ISBN: 978-1-7387599-2-7).

29. The Diefenbunker – Canadian Forces Station Carp - really exists. It was built in 1959 through 1961, opened in 1962, and remained operational until it was closed and decommissioned in 1994. It has since been designated a National Historic Site of Canada and reopened as a museum in 1998. *See* https://diefenbunker.ca/en/. For Alex's adventure involving the Diefenbunker see *An Ineradicable Mountie* ((ISBN: 978-1-7387599-2-7).

30. In the Security Service, at this time in history, the sections were denoted with letters A through L: 'A', for security screening, 'B', for counter-espionage, 'C' for administration, 'D', for counter-subversion (or anti-communism), 'E' for electronic surveillance, 'F' for files, 'G' for counter-terrorism (absorbed into D Section in 1976), 'H' for China, 'I' for physical surveillance, 'J' for bugging, and 'L' for informants. According to Sawatsky (See endnote #8): *"As far as is known, there is no K Section. For some reason the letters jump from J to L. One Security*

Service member theorized that K Section may exist but plays such a minor role that nobody knows about it. 'Either that,' he joked, 'or it exists and is very important'." Other accounts suggest that this section was for research. Since there is some mystery about whether 'K' Section actually existed, or it's purpose if it did exist, I have made it 'Special Operations,' hence very important, in these novels.

31. See *An Indestructible Mountie* (ISBN: 978-1-9994940-4-9).
32. The Cambridge Five was a ring of Soviet spies operating in the United Kingdom between the 1930s and '50s. Most of them held sensitive positions in MI5, MI6, or the Foreign Office.
33. J. Edgar Hoover was the founding Director of the U.S. Federal Bureau of Investigation (FBI) and served from 1935 to 1972. Hoover's main preoccupation was with communist subversion, whether real or perceived.
34. See *An Inseparable Mountie* (ISBN: 978-1-7772424-0-4).
35. See *An Intrepid Mountie* (ISBN: 978-1-7772424-6-6).
36. A cryptonym is a code word or name used to refer to something else without revealing its true identity. The something else, could be almost anything, including a person, word or phrase, project, or object.
37. The main organizational units within the Security Service were variously known as Sections, Branches, Operations, or simply Ops.
38. The 'Five Eyes' is an intelligence-sharing alliance among Canada, Australia, New Zealand, the U.K., and the U.S. It seems to have begun with a signals- and code-breaking alliance during the Second World War, and then expanded during the Cold War to include intelligence generally. It is still active in the present day.
39. This was the National Research Universal (NRU) reactor. A fuel rod ruptured, causing a fire and subsequent contamination of the reactor building.
40. In 1945, Soviet cipher clerk Igor Gouzenko abandoned his position with the Soviet Embassy in Ottawa and defected to Canada, bringing with him more than a hundred documents showing that a Soviet spy network was operating in Canada. This sparked an international crisis, because the network targeted people working in sensitive positions with access to military, scientific, and other secrets. The affair remained alive

for nearly twenty years due to investigations, a Royal Commission, 21 arrests, and 20 trials leading to ten convictions in Canada and one in the UK.

41. This was the second Canada Cup. It had originally been scheduled for 1979 but went off due to disputes between Hockey Canada and the Canadian Amateur Hockey Association. Although rescheduled for 1980, this too collapsed due to Canada's boycotts in response to the Soviet Union's invasion of Afghanistan. Rescheduled a third time, it finally took place September 1–13, 1981.

42. The Montreal Forum (*Forum de Montreal*), the original home of the Montreal Canadiens, was arguably the most famous arena in hockey history. It opened in 1924 and was closed in 1996. Although the exterior of the historic building remains standing, it was gutted in 1998 and rebuilt to house movie theatres and a restaurant.

43. The 'nosebleeds' is a slang reference to the seats in the very highest, and therefore cheapest, rows of a hockey arena. In the old Montreal Forum, the nosebleeds were so high up that it was almost impossible to see the puck on the ice.

44. See *An Ineradicable Mountie* (ISBN: 978-1-7387599-2-7).

45. See *An Inseparable Mountie* (ISBN: 978-1-7772424-0-4).

46. See *An Intrepid Mountie* (ISBN: 978-1-7772424-6-6).

47. See *An Ineradicable Mountie* (ISBN: 978-1-7387599-2-7).

48. In August, 1980, when the Czechoslovakian team was playing in a tournament in Innsbruck, Austria, two of their star players, Peter and Anton Stastny (Šťastný), defected after the final game by driving to Canadian Embassy in Vienna, after which, with a police escort they made their way to the airport and flew to Canada where they joined the Québec Nordiques. A year later their oldest brother, Marian, defected as well, also to join the Nordiques.

49. See *An Inimitable Mountie* (ISBN: 978-1-0690565-0-4).

50. In real life, at the time of this story, Canadian Forces uniforms were not exactly as described due to a 1968 government initiative called unification, under which the various services were merged with unified commands, common rank designations, and common uniforms, the latter in rifle green. As time passed, some elements of unification were rescinded. In the late 1980s, for example the traditional air force and navy

uniform colours were restored. In 2011, some of the more traditional command names were also restored, such as for the Royal Canadian Air Force (RCAF). In the fictional world of this novel series, however, unification never took place.

51. The RCAF's C-130H Hercules are four-engine-turboprop, tactical-transport aircraft. Designed to operate from low quality, short airstrips, they have been used for everything from troop and equipment transport, to search and rescue, and even air-to-air refueling operations.

52. Canadian Forces Base Trenton, located in southern Ontario, is home to 8 Wing, which provides tactical transportation worldwide and supports search and rescue operations over central and northern Canada.

53. At the time of this story, noise-cancelling headphones hadn't been invented yet. Amar Bose, the founder of Bose Corporation, invented the first portable noise-cancelling headphone in 1989, and they only became widely available to the public in 2000.

54. Canadian Special Passports have a green cover and are issued to Senators, Members of Parliament, and government people in a non-diplomatic capacity that are travelling to a post abroad and/or on an official mission.

55. Several Boeing 707-347C aircraft were built for the RCAF and designated CC-137. Built in passenger and tanker versions, the former was used for long-range passenger transport, and particularly VIP transport, between 1970 and 1997.

56. In real life, the practice of referring to the head of MI6 as "C" dates back to Capt. Sir Mansfield George Smith-Cumming, RN, who became the head of the UK's Secret Service Bureau in the early 1900s and the first head of the renamed Secret Intelligence Service (MI6). Even before becoming head, he became known to insiders as 'C,' due to his habit of signing letters and documents (in green ink) with a C. Both the initial and the green ink became a tradition for later heads of MI6, for whom the C stands for 'Chief.' In fiction writing, the former intelligence officers John Le Carré called his MI6 chief 'Control,' while Ian Fleming called his 'M.'

57. Experts. Often scientists or engineers.

58. (a) Gideon was a prophet, judge, and military leader in both the Hebrew and Christian Bibles. (b) Gideons International is an

Evangelical Christian association founded in the late 1800s, in the United States. They are best known for placing free bibles in hotel and motel rooms, the original idea for which seems to have been to engage traveling salespeople in evangelism. Since then, the Gideons have distributed billions of Bibles worldwide.

59. At the time of this story, MI6 (the UK's Secret Intelligence Service) had its headquarters at Century House, on Westminster Bridge Road in London. This building was used by them from 1964 to 1994. Its location was at one time an official secret, but ultimately became so widely known that it was declassified shortly before the service's headquarters moved to its present-day location.

60. The London Underground (also known simply as the Underground or by its nickname the Tube) is a rapid transit (electric train) system, only about half of which is actually underground.

61. In Ian Fleming's James Bond novels, Miss Moneypenny, was the personal assistant for the head of MI6.

62. In real life as well, MI6 seems to be about the only part of the UK government that has been able to avoid having to transfer any their records to the national registry. See www.nationalarchives.gov.uk.

63. The M203 is a single-shot under-barrel grenade launcher designed to attach to a rifle. It was introduced in the 1970s, and can fire a variety of types of 40 mm rounds ranging from high-explosive, to star-shell, to CS (o-chlorobenzylidene malononitrile) tear gas grenades.

64. The RCMP's H Division is responsible for federal policing in Nova Scotia, and B Division for Newfoundland and Labrador.

65. The NATO M549 is a high-explosive, rocket-assisted 155 mm howitzer round. It has a maximum range of about 30 km.

66. *HMCS Assiniboine* (DDH 234), the second ship to bear this name, served in the Royal Canadian Navy between 1956 to 1988. She was the second ship to bear the name. A St. Laurent-class destroyer, she was converted to a destroyer-helicopter-escort in 1962 and spent much of her service as an anti-submarine ship patrolling the western North Atlantic.

67. 'The penny dropped,' is an old expression meaning that something has suddenly, or finally, become recognized or

understood. It seems to have originated in Britain, in the late 1800s, when there was a proliferation of automatic machines that could be activated by the inserting (dropping) of a penny into a slot (including vending machines, gas meters, and almost-instant photo machines). In all cases, the desired action didn't happen until the penny dropped.

68. AIS, the VHS-radio-based Automatic Identification System, by which vessels are required to continuously broadcast their identity and position, wasn't developed until the 1990s. Similarly, although the first practical GPS (Global Positioning System) satellite was launched in 1978, it wasn't until the first large network of GPS satellites was launched in the early 1990s that GPS became fully functional.

69. The KH-9 (codename HEXAGON; also known as Big Bird) refers to a program of photographic-reconnaissance satellites used by the U.S. in the 1970s and '80s. Each satellite generally carried two main cameras. When rolls of film from the cameras were full, they were sent to one of four re-entry vehicles and jettisoned.

70. The RA-5C Vigilante was a reconnaissance version of the U.S. Navy's A-5 aircraft-carrier-based, all-weather, supersonic bomber. The RA-5Cs were in active service between 1963 and 1980.

71. *USCGC Decisive* (WMEC-629) was a Reliance-Class, medium-endurance U.S. Coast Guard Cutter. At the time of this story, she probably carried a Sikorsky HH-52 Seaguard helicopter. She was decommissioned in 2023.

72. Georges Island is a small island in Halifax's inner harbour; almost directly offshore Pier 21. Located on the island is an operating lighthouse, which was originally established in 1876, rebuilt in 1917, and automated in 1972. Also located on the island is Fort Charlotte, which was constructed in 1750 and played various defensive roles up to an including the Second World War. Georges Island is now a National Historic Site.

73. On July 2, 1981, the *HMCS Assiniboine* ran aground in Halifax Harbour in heavy fog, requiring the aid from several tugboats to get free.

74. The Richmond Terminals, formerly the Richmond Yards, date back to the first railway in Halifax. This site is very close to where, on December 6., 1917, the out-bound freighter *Imo*

collided with the munitions-freighter *Mont Blanc*, which was heading in-bound for the Bedford Basin. The collision yielded the massive "Halifax Explosion," which levelled approximately five square kilometres of the city. At the Richmond Yards, two of its piers were badly damaged and another two were completely destroyed by the blast. *See* D. Smith, "The Railways and Canada's Greatest Disaster: The Halifax Explosion, December 6, 1917," *Canadian Rail* 431(Nov./Dec.) 202–212 (1992).

75. A derivative of "There is no peace for the weary," or "There is no peace for the wicked," meaning that one must keep on working no matter how tired they are. The original quote is probably from the Bible: "There is no peace for the wicked" (*Isaiah* 48:22 and 57:21), referring to eternal punishment.

76. David Cornwell, a former MI5, then MI6 officer (better known as the author of espionage novels under his pen-name of John Le Carré) interviewed a close friend of Kim Philby, the long-standing MI6 officer and Soviet double agent who later defected to the Soviet Union. As a result, Cornwell/Le Carré concluded that: "What may have begun as an ideological commitment became a psychological dependency, then a craving. One side wasn't enough for him. He needed to play the world's game... when Philby was... living out the inglorious end of his career as an MI6 and KGB agent... what he missed most... was the prickle of the double life that had for so long sustained him." See J. Le Carré, *"The Pigeon Tunnel. Stories from My Life,"* Penguin Canada, Toronto, 2017, p. 176.

77. The original *Mission: Impossible* television series was broadcast by CBS between 1966 and 1973. It featured the espionage exploits of a team of U.S. Government secret agents called the Impossible Missions Force.

78. Long service in the RCMP is recognized by the awarding of a star for each five years of service. The embroidered stars are sewn onto the left sleeve of the red- and brown serge tunics.

79. Prior to 1946, in the RCMP, domestic intelligence and security matters were handled by the Criminal Investigation Branch. Such work was moved to the newly created Special Branch in 1946, to which was added responsibility for counter-intelligence operations. In 1956, the Special Branch was renamed Directorate of Security and Intelligence. In 1970, it

became the Security Service. The Security Service was later absorbed by the new and independent Canadian Security Intelligence Service (CSIS) in 1984.

80. In real life, there have been Cold-War-traitors within the RCMP Security Service. In the 1950s, there was agent 'Gideon,' a Soviet agent that was turned and run as a double agent, plus another officer that sold-out Gideon to the Soviets. The mid-1960s brought a very public case that led to the Mackenzie Royal Commission on Security. There have also been some unsuccessful mole hunts, such as operation 'Feather Bed,' that ultimately turned up no one, and operation 'Gridiron,' that landed on the wrong person. Similar things happened in the U.S. and Britain. See: R. Whitaker, "Spies Who Might Have Been: Canada and the Myth of Cold War Counterintelligence," *Intelligence and National Security*, 12(4), 25-43, 2008.

81. In the 1960s and '70s, there was a movement for Québec independence from which grew an urban-terrorist group called *Front de libération du Québec* (FLQ). With regard to the RCMP Security Service's activities in the events leading up to, and following the 'October Crisis' of 1970, it found itself under attack from two very different directions. On the one hand, a number of federal Cabinet Ministers – including the Prime Minister – complained that the intelligence gathered by the Security Service was inadequate, if not worse. On the other hand, the service was publicly attacked for going too far in its efforts, some of which were labelled unethical and/or unlawful. In August 1981, a commission of inquiry into the operations and policies of the RCMP Security Service, known as the McDonald Commission, recommended civilianization, meaning a civilian security intelligence agency, separate from the RCMP and without law-enforcement powers, should be created. This was eventually accomplished in the *Canadian Security Intelligence Service Act* of 1984.

Laurie Schramm

ADVENTURES OF THE FIRST WOMAN MOUNTIE

www.laurieschramm.ca

www.facebook.com/LaurieSchrammBooks

Laurie Schramm

Laurie Schramm